Miguel, the slight Puerto Rican who was one of the building's handymen, was almost hidden by the huge bouquet. "Señora, she is beautiful flowers."

"Indeed they are," Dianne said, and took the bundle, slipping a couple of dollars into his hand. "Thank you so much, Miguel." She supposed the flowers were from Charlie, a sort of apology for entertaining Zoe and leaving her alone. . . .

She closed the door and carried the flowers to her little arranging room off the kitchen. Stripping away the paper, she found a mass of fragrant lilies, as well as roses, carnations, daisies, sweet peas, with some baby's breath and greens. Then she gasped. Mixed in with the live flowers were clumps of dead blooms, ugly dried flowers, emitting a subtle, nauseating stench. . . .

Then she saw the card. . . .

By Joyce Christmas
Published by Fawcett Books:

Lady Margaret Priam mysteries:
A FÊTE WORSE THAN DEATH
SUDDENLY IN HER SORBET
SIMPLY TO DIE FOR
A STUNNING WAY TO DIE
FRIEND OR FAUX
IT'S HER FUNERAL
A PERFECT DAY FOR DYING
MOURNING GLORIA
GOING OUT IN STYLE

Betty Trenka mysteries:
THIS BUSINESS IS MURDER
DEATH AT FACE VALUE
DOWNSIZED TO DEATH

GOING OUT IN STYLE

A Lady Margaret Priam Mystery

Joyce Christmas

FAWCETT GOLD MEDAL • NEW YORK

A Fawcett Gold Medal Book
Published by The Ballantine Publishing Group
Copyright © 1998 by Joyce Christmas

All rights reserved under International and Pan-American Copyright Conventions. Published in the United States by The Ballantine Publishing Group, a division of Random House, Inc., New York, and simultaneously in Canada by Random House of Canada Limited, Toronto.

http://www.randomhouse.com

Library of Congress Catalog Number: 97-95352

ISBN: 0-449-15010-0

Manufactured in the United States of America

First Edition: June 1998

10 9 8 7 6 5 4 3 2 1

For all treasured friends,
you know who you are.
And here's to one of the best,
Kate Grilley

Chapter 1

"*I want* to go back to work." Dianne Stark, former airline hostess/cabin crew member/stewardess, poured herself another cup of smoky Lapsang Souchong tea, and would not meet Lady Margaret Priam's surprised eye.

Afternoon tea at the Villa d'Este hotel off Manhattan's Park Avenue was a favorite ritual of Margaret's, if only because somehow the volatile Italian chef managed to offer seedcake and delicate watercress sandwiches that reminded her of teatime back home in England, in the big, comfortable drawing room of Priam's Priory, with her mother, the late Countess of Brayfield, presiding. Nowadays, of course, her brother, the present earl, preferred his tea taken in a heavy mug in the old arched room that the monks who had long ago inhabited the old priory had used as their refectory. She supposed—or rather hoped—that if David ever married, his wife would return tea to the drawing room, where it properly belonged.

"Work? What sort of work? Why?" This was the first time Margaret had heard Dianne mention going back to work, although they were ostensibly great friends and confidantes. Dianne fidgeted in the elegant but uncomfortable chair. She was in her early thirties, only a year or two younger than Margaret, and she was slim and glamorous,

1

as befitted the trophy wife (and much more) of financier
Charles Stark, who was considerably her senior and who,
from all reports and Margaret's own observation, doted
on her.

Margaret looked at Dianne's uncharacteristically sober
expression, and realized that there was a lot she didn't
know about her friend. It was easy to assume Charlie's
devotion from Dianne's comments and from seeing them
together at social events and at home, but was it true? Dianne never spoke much about her marriage. She'd heard
Dianne's tales from her airline years, and reminiscences
from her rather ordinary but happy childhood, even the
usual horror stories about gross high school dates, disastrous proms and the like. They'd had quite a laugh about
the time the elastic on her panties gave way as Dianne
was approaching the stage at a high school assembly. "I
followed my mother's advice," Dianne had said. " 'Just
kick them aside and pretend nothing had happened.' So I
did."

But it was a flimsy anecdotal net, nothing you could
wrap around yourself and feel the substance of a life.

Even wearing a troubled look, Dianne remained a stunning figure in the d'Este's flattering lighting. She'd had
her hairdresser cut her hair short and add a few russet
highlights. With her new curly hair, she looked different,
almost boyish. Her makeup was, as always, perfect. Only
a year earlier, she and Charlie had become parents of a
delightful little boy, which pleased Charlie, who already
had, Margaret seemed to recall, at least one grown off-
spring from a previous marriage.

"Don't you have plenty to do caring for the infant?"
Margaret thought the mention of little Chip might erase

the fatigued look from Dianne's lovely oval face. Instead she looked more troubled.

"We have the nanny," Dianne said in a low, uninflected voice. She fiddled with a spoon and frowned. "Charlie insisted so I would be free for"—she waved her hand to encompass her sedate surroundings—"all this. Whatever I wanted to do. Lourdes pretty much has full charge of him, and she's very reliable, although I hope he won't speak English with a Filipino accent." Then she added hastily, "I do spend a lot of time with him. Really. I put him to bed and read him stories. He doesn't understand all that much, but he likes the pictures, and he likes songs and things. Of course, Charlie's seen to it that he has lovely toys. . . ."

A passing waiter brushed against Dianne's chair, and she reacted with a gasp, drawing back in near terror. The spoon clattered to the floor, and Dianne retrieved it with a trembling hand.

"Pardon, signora," the waiter said. He was Italian, of course, and young, but blond. Probably from Northern Italy, Margaret decided. "So clumsy . . ." His distress was evident. Clumsiness was not tolerated at the Villa d'Este.

"Not to worry," Margaret said, and leaned toward Dianne. "What's the matter? You're all nerves today."

"Nothing's the matter. We were talking about my busy, purposeful days." It wasn't hard to hear the sarcasm in her voice. "Besides Chip, I have my good works and charity committees to occupy me. Well, you know that. You're on practically all the same ones. But they're not . . . not . . ."

"Meaningful?" Margaret ventured. Each committee she'd gotten involved with seemed to have brought out the worst in everyone. At least two had ended up with someone dead, which was certainly meaningful to the deceased, and could be considered meaningful to the survivors, especially if they were mentioned in the will, but she understood what Dianne meant.

"What good does it really do to raise a couple thousand dollars for a charity, when we committee members put in many more thousands in effort alone?" Dianne leaned across the table, but Margaret noticed she glanced quickly from side to side first, as if looking for someone. "I could go back with the airlines, you know. I got my weight down after the baby, and I'm not too old. I wouldn't have the seniority I'd have had if I'd kept working, but still. I miss seeing all those different cities. You know, places where no one can find me." Dianne didn't look at all well, and certainly not happy. Even the carefully applied makeup didn't mask the hint of the dark circles under her eyes.

"Dianne, darling. Thanks to Charlie, you're rich. You can fly to any city you want anytime you want to. Charlie wouldn't keep you from a weekend in San Francisco, or London, or Paris. He adores you, and he'd probably go with you. The infant has that nanny to mind him. You say she's a dream come true, so you wouldn't have a care in the world."

"It's not the same," Dianne said with a stubborn look. "I feel so . . . so exposed in New York. And the other thing is, I hate taking money from Charlie. He just throws a lot of dollars into my bank account. I don't even spend it. I keep it handy in case I need it for emergencies. He pays all my credit card charges without a whimper. I'd like to have my very own money that I actually earned, the way I used to. Even if it's not very much."

"You're just feeling restless," Margaret said. "It's because it's spring at last. Maybe you should do a big tiring spring cleaning, and get all this out of your system."

The Starks' vast apartment in a very nice building on the corner of Fifth Avenue and a quiet cross street was not a place Margaret herself would lightly have undertaken the spring cleaning of, but it might be just the thing for Dianne.

"We have the housekeeper," Dianne said, "and she brings in whatever help she needs to clean. She buys groceries, does the cooking, everything. But she does let me arrange the flowers. I have a little room off the kitchen with vases and scissors and florist's wire, everything I need. I started a flower-arranging course, but dropped it. I've been in touch with the personnel department of my old airline. They say I could go back. You should understand. You're always looking for work."

That was true. Since Bedros Kasparian had closed his antiques shop, where she'd been his sales assistant, her jobs had not been enormously profitable. It was not easy being an English aristocrat in New York without an immense fortune to buy the nice things she liked. She did not have much wealth, although she wasn't starving, but she certainly didn't have a Charles Stark to shower her with dollars. At present she was working with a much-in-demand interior designer, soothing his anxious clients with her upper-class English accent and undeniable good taste, while Giovanni charged them substantial sums to have their walls stripped and repainted just the right shade of off-white, and to help them select the perfect chair. But then, if she and Sam De Vere finally managed to marry, things would be different again. Sam would retire from the New York Police, and they'd move to some dreadful suburb. She'd have to stop fetching and carrying for Giovanni, and even that small income would be gone. She did understand Dianne's feelings. It would be hateful to expect Sam to pay for her manicures, or to tell her that they couldn't afford the designer frock she'd fallen in love with.

"So the wife of the distinguished Charles Stark will be found on board a big silver bird, headed for distant shores, all the while handing out hot towels and bad coffee . . ."

Dianne gazed up at the elaborate Italianate gilt ceiling for a moment. "No," she said finally and sadly, "even if I talk about it, I know I can't go back to that life. I couldn't leave Charlie and the baby like that. Even if they'd be safer without me around. I just feel I've got to do something worthwhile. More worthwhile than having my hair done and arranging flowers, lunching with friends . . . and enemies . . ."

"You don't have an enemy in the world. And exactly what do you mean by 'safer'?"

Dianne dismissed that question except to say, "Maybe I do have enemies. You just don't know about him . . . them." Dianne slumped in the chair, she who always displayed perfect posture. Margaret was beginning seriously to worry about her, if she were imagining enemies and concerned about her family's safety.

"All right," Dianne conceded finally. "Not enemies exactly, but uncongenials. I hate it when Madame Chair Lady running this or that worthy cause rants at me about how slow ticket sales are to the next gala. As if it was my fault that people don't want to cough up a thousand dollars for watery cocktails and another boring meal featuring chicken. And I feel so false checking Poppy Dill's column dutifully to see if she mentioned that Charlie and

I attended this ball or that one, or whether my name is featured prominently when it should be."

"Poppy loves to mention you," Margaret said. And it was true that the Starks, Dianne especially, were favorites of the aging society columnist, whose "Social Scene" column appeared several times a week in one of the city's tabloid newspapers, recounting the follies and fantasies of the cream of New York society.

"I don't care about being mentioned," Dianne said. Then she added, "Poppy's column is what started it all."

"All what?"

Dianne squirmed and shrugged. "Oh, feeling not valuable, unproductive, just another glossy face and glossy name to titillate the masses. Even having the baby doesn't make me feel valuable, except when I manage to teach him something new. And Charlie is so busy these days that the only good I do him is being his hostess when he invites his associates around. There are only a couple of people who truly value me . . ." Dianne had an odd look suddenly, a sort of ironic half smile on her lips, then the frown returned. "There's you, of course, and maybe one or two others."

Something clicked, and Margaret sat up and leaned forward. "Are you telling me that you have a . . . a beau?"

"Certainly not!" Dianne answered too quickly, and Margaret wasn't convinced. It was all too common in their circles for attractive women with terribly busy husbands and not enough else to do to take a lover, especially when the woman was as well-off as Dianne. The Stark fortune, her many social assets, and undeniable beauty made her a ready and tempting target for amorous society hangers-on.

"Well, you can tell me if you want," Margaret said. "It won't go beyond my ears. You know you can trust me."

"I know I can, and I may have to someday. But there's nothing to tell right now," Dianne said, looking restless and uncomfortable and again glancing quickly from side to side. However, there was nobody in sight in the tearoom except the blond waiter and an aged Italian countess who was probably a relative of Prince Aldo Castrocani, the former husband of Carolyn Sue Hoopes, the owner of the Villa d'Este. "I should be getting home. Charlie said he was leaving the office early today, to take me out to dinner."

"Now, that's nice," Margaret said.

"Not really," Dianne said with a trace of bitterness. "We're going with a colleague of his and his wife to Doubles or some such place, where everything is decorous and comfortable, and business can be discussed by the gentlemen while the wife and I natter on about the servant problem and the baby. She already has grandchildren, so she can give me good advice on child-rearing that I don't want to hear. Then my sister is coming to visit today. Actually, she'll be staying indefinitely, I'm afraid, and she's high maintenance, so I have to start thinking of ways to entertain her." She looked at Margaret hopefully. "I know you said that Paul is engaged, but maybe he has a friend for her?"

"He's not back from the Caribbean yet, but he's coming home soon." Dianne had once dreamed of hooking up her younger sister with Prince Paul Castrocani, Carolyn Sue's son. "I'll ask him." Margaret remembered meeting Karen on another visit to New York. She was as pretty as Dianne, and looked very much like her, but Margaret had known at once that she and Paul would not make a match.

She had seemed as devoted to finding a mate with money as Paul was, and Margaret recalled some envious digs at Dianne for having managed to snare the wealthy Charlie.

"I'll think of something for her to do," Dianne said wearily. "Maybe one of my rumored admirers will take a fancy to her. I'll see what I can arrange. It might please her to think she's taken someone away from me again." Dianne hesitated. "I must have told you about the time . . ." She stopped, although Margaret was eager to hear. Then she signaled to the waiter, who was promptly at the table. "Campari and soda." To Margaret she said, "Care for something stronger than tea? I have to get myself in a mellower frame of mind for . . . for going home and dinner, and seeing that Karen's room will be to her liking."

"The tea is fine," Margaret said, and ate another watercress sandwich. Dianne was not a drinker, although a gentle aperitif like Campari was not truly drinking. No, and playing cards for a few cents a point wasn't truly gambling. "I wish you'd tell me what's troubling you. I know something is. You're not behaving like yourself."

"I don't know who 'myself' is anymore. I'm feeling useless, and my life is pointless. Having Karen around isn't going to help, but what could I do? She's decided she wants to live in New York. And don't start about the baby and Charlie. You won't give me any arguments I haven't already gone over and over."

Margaret looked her in the eye, and Dianne responded sharply, "And I don't have a lover, so don't start on that. You know I'd tell you if I did. I just . . . I just . . ."

Margaret was afraid that Dianne was on the brink of tears. The waiter placed a tall glass full of soda and pink Campari in front of her.

"Thank you so much." Dianne recovered and was again an elegant, cool lady of grace and substance. "I have to run as soon as I've finished this." She drank the Campari thirstily. "Charlie hates me to be late when his business associates are involved. But I don't like to be too predictable. I shouldn't even have gone out today." She put down the empty glass and opened her handbag.

"I'll put it on my house account," Margaret said. "Carolyn Sue arranged for me to have one here."

"Thanks," Dianne said. "My treat next time, if there is a next time." She stood up and actually looked quite animated. "Margaret, please, please join us for dinner tonight. I need you. It's George and Emily Armitage. You like her, don't you?"

What was a friend to do? "Of course, Dianne."

"It will be eightish. I'll call with the name of the place."

Margaret watched her walk away from the table, hesitate at the door, and peer out into the dim lobby as though she were expecting to see someone behind the potted palms. Margaret was puzzled and not a little unnerved by Dianne's behavior. She was going to get to the bottom of it. It's what any good friend would do. Maybe Dianne should be persuaded to take another course in flower arranging, if that was what interested her. Or an exercise class. Margaret had been thinking about joining a health club, so they could join together.

Margaret signed the bill, and tried to forget about Dianne's trembling hand and look of distress. But she couldn't forget that however comfortable she felt in Dianne's company, she had no real grasp of the woman's inner life. Then she wondered if perhaps the shallow, social life Dianne had complained about and which she too led was draining away her understanding of her fellow human beings. How often in the past half-dozen years since she'd arrived here from England and befriended Dianne had she really asked Dianne how she felt and what she thought? Not often. Mostly they just giggled about the follies of their fellow committee members. Or mocked a disastrous dress or a failed face-lift.

"I will be a better friend," Margaret vowed to no one except herself, and proceeded from the Villa d'Este, with only a glance at the sleek waiter who was admiring her blond hair and nicely turned ankle.

Chapter 2

The restaurant Charles Stark had chosen was located in a charming East Side carriage house, not far from Margaret's apartment building. She was glad it wasn't a high-profile dining experience like Le Cirque 2000 or the Four Seasons, but a comfortable and even romantic spot.

She was the first to arrive, and she hated that, but the staff had Charlie's reservation. She was seated at once and served a lovely sherry, just as Emily and George Armitage arrived. Margaret had been pleased to learn that the Armitages would be the other couple. Although she knew them only slightly, Emily was quite a well-known novelist and critic who never let convention stand in the way of her convictions.

The maître d' guided them to the table.

"I hope you don't mind my intrusion," Margaret said. "Dianne begged me to join you."

"Delighted to have you, Lady Margaret," George said. "I hope you won't be bored with the conversation. Charlie and I are making this rather a business meeting, since I am off to London tomorrow."

"I'm sure Emily and Dianne and I can entertain ourselves," Margaret said.

"We'll concentrate on the food," Emily said. "The chef

here is quite accomplished. Ah, here's Charlie and Dianne now. What a lovely couple . . ." Her voice trailed off oddly, and Margaret looked toward the entrance.

Charles Stark looked prosperous and self-satisfied as usual, and Dianne, clinging to his arm, seemed fragile but glowing as she looked up at his face and laughed.

"Oh, dear," Margaret said, and peered at the couple more intently.

It was not Dianne on Charlie's arm, but her sister Karen, who looked enough like Dianne to fool a casual observer.

"Evening, everyone," Charles said. "George, Emily—I don't believe you know my sister-in-law, Karen Reid. I think Margaret and Karen are acquainted."

"Margaret! How nice to see you again," Karen said. "Poor Dianne was feeling under the weather. She's been very nervy lately, have you noticed? So I offered to be Charlie's date. She didn't mention that you'd be here."

"Hullo, Karen. She must have forgotten she asked me to come along." They seated themselves, and Margaret noticed that Karen arranged to be seated between Charlie and George.

"She's very forgetful lately," Charlie said. "And imagining all sorts of things. I've insisted that she see a specialist, someone who doesn't just give her tranquilizers and think he's solved the problem. Well, Emily, you're looking charming tonight."

Emily Armitage was a solid, no-nonsense woman with short gray hair, and not especially charming to look at, but she seemed to appreciate Charlie's compliment.

"Em's been struggling along with the new book," George said. "The only way I can get a decent meal is to go out to places like this." He started to peruse the menu with care.

"No great chunks of steak for you," Emily warned. "I don't want to be a widow because you choose to over-indulge in carnivorous feasts."

"What a sad thing," Karen said. The table looked at her expectantly.

"To be a widow, or a widower. I mean, it's so sad to be left alone." She looked at Charlie coyly, and it seemed to Margaret that her hand beneath the table was touching his. It made her feel distinctly uncomfortable. Even Emily appeared to notice.

Charlie leaned across Karen to speak to George in a low voice. "Karen, why don't you change places with George so that he and Charlie can get on with their business?" Emily said briskly.

Karen hesitated, then arranged to change places with Charlie, so she was still seated beside him.

"That's better," Emily said. But not much, Margaret thought. "Are you going to be visiting in New York for a while?"

"As long as I can, maybe forever," Karen said. "You can't imagine how dull Rhode Island is. I work at a bank in Providence, but I'd much prefer to be in New York with my family." Again the fluttered eyelashes in Charlie's direction, but he was deeply into his discussion with George and didn't seem to notice. "Charlie is going to look around and help me make some connections. Oh, Margaret, maybe that darling Prince Paul could help. He's a banker, isn't he?"

"In a manner of speaking," Margaret said, knowing that Paul had not been a resounding success at United National, "but I'm afraid he's not in the city at the moment, although he's coming back from the Caribbean quite soon."

"Dianne says that he's engaged, so I guess there's no hope for little me." She'd now placed her hand on Charlie's shoulder in a cool, possessive manner. This time he did turn to her and smile.

"None," Margaret said shortly, and wondered how two sisters could be so different. Dianne was never such an obvious schemer.

"Charlie's going to see about an apartment, too, but his place is so huge, one more person in the place doesn't make much difference. And he has servants and the car whenever I need it. We're going to have such fun. If Dianne will just get over what's ailing her."

Emily Armitage was gazing at Karen with a bemused expression. "What exactly *is* ailing her?"

"Oh, she has some idea that someone is following her. She's always been kind of a nut, ever since we were kids. Sisters know sisters pretty well."

"Now, that interests me," Emily said. "My new book deals with sisters."

"You write books? How fascinating! I often think I'd like to write a book, if only I could find the time."

Margaret could tell that Emily was holding back a sharp, perhaps sarcastic comment. Then she said, "Time is what it takes, dear. Tell me about your relationship with your sister. You can never have enough insights."

"There's not much to tell. I was a couple of years younger than she, and I wanted to be like her. She was so pretty and popular. So I used to steal her makeup and stuff, borrow her clothes. She always said she wanted to die young and well dressed, so she had the nicest clothes. Sometimes we'd have fights about boys and not speak to each other for ages. Then she grew up and got married. That didn't work out, but he was a cute guy."

Margaret thought she must have misheard. Dianne had never mentioned a prior marriage, but Karen burbled on, and the moment to question her was lost.

"Not as cute as my Charlie baby, though." Karen had a complacent expression on her face and a proprietary tone in her voice.

Charles may not have heard what she was saying, but he looked away from George to Karen at the sound of his name. Margaret didn't like his expression, sort of moony and indulgent.

"Dianne," Emily said sharply, "I mean, Karen. I suppose you'll join Dianne in her various charitable ventures. She does so much good."

"Borrrring," Karen said. "I want to see all the shops and the clothes and shoes. There's plenty of time to do good later, when . . . when we're settled." ·

"Here's dinner," Emily said with some relief. "I'm famished." George didn't seem terribly happy with his broiled fish, but he had taken his wife's warning to heart.

The food was delicious, and it was less stressful to eat than to watch Karen cozy up to Charlie.

After coffee the two men wandered to the cigar-bar part of the restaurant.

"George insists on smoking one of those awful things every evening," Emily said.

To Margaret's astonishment Karen went with them, arm-in-arm with both Charlie and George.

"That's a dangerous young woman," Emily said. "I hope the bonds of sisterhood can withstand . . ."

"I wonder," Margaret said. "Should I warn Dianne?"

"In my experience," Emily said, "a sister has a pretty good idea of what the other is up to. If Karen seems dangerous now, she's probably always been dangerous, and I think Dianne is bright enough to realize it."

"Dianne said that her sister was high maintenance. I only hope the price isn't too high."

Chapter 3

Two days later Margaret called Dianne to confirm a committee meeting both were to attend and to suggest the exercise class. The phone seemed to ring for an extraordinarily long time before an answering machine picked up.

"Dianne, it's me, Margaret. Please pick up if you're there, or else call me about the Bountiful Harvest committee."

Dianne was suddenly on the line, sounding breathless. "Margaret, I'm sorry. I've gotten into the habit of screening calls. I don't allow Lourdes or the housekeeper to answer, but I was afraid my sister would pick up. I usually just wait for the machine to switch on."

"Not a problem," Margaret said. "I do it myself. How is Karen managing her new life in New York?"

"I don't like the way she takes up so much of Charlie's time. He never has a moment for Chip."

"Things will be different when she gets a job," Margaret said.

"She'll sponge off of us for as long as Charlie will tolerate it. I think it's her way of getting even with me for . . . for everything."

"Look, Dianne, I called to ask if you would be at the meeting tomorrow. It really *is* a worthwhile cause. All that food bought for the homeless and shut-ins. And it will be a fun party when we get it all organized. Sam has even agreed to attend, and you know how he avoids my social events. You could bring your sister to the committee meeting and the party."

"I . . . I can't come to the meeting," Dianne said. "And I don't want Karen to start thinking she's some kind of society star, hobnobbing with those rich silly women, who will just put ideas in her head. There's something else I have to do. I'll call Elinor and apologize. She'll be furious. She seems to think that being chair lady renders the rest of us her slaves. And she's been especially testy with me for some reason." Margaret heard another phone ringing. The Starks had several phone lines, but presumably several answering machines.

"Pick up your other call," Margaret said. "Let's do lunch soon, after the committee meeting, so I can tell you all the gossip. Your sister could join us for that at least. I didn't have much chance to talk with her at dinner the other night."

"Emily said she was all over Charlie and George," Dianne said. "That's just like her. She fancies older men, and she's always been luxury-minded with not too many other thoughts in her head. I don't like the way she's talking Charlie into bankrolling her fashion adventures, as though it was her right as my sister. I've simply got to get back to work, or she'll drive me crazy."

Margaret didn't like the sound of that. "In any event," Margaret said, "I have some thoughts I want to share before you pack your flight bag." The other phone continued to ring. "Get your call."

"I don't want to talk to anybody," Dianne said, and then shouted at the empty ringing behind her. "You can call and call, and you'll never speak to me." Then Dianne ended Margaret's call without a good-bye.

Margaret sat with the receiver in her hand for a long minute, puzzled about the usually even-tempered Dianne. It was more than simply feeling useless and finding committee business worthless, Margaret was certain. There was too much emotional turmoil leaking out through cracks in Dianne's typically controlled facade. It couldn't all be Karen's intrusion. Then she dialed Poppy Dill.

"Poppy, do you have a few minutes?" If there was a problem in the Starks' marriage, Poppy would have heard the little gusts of rumor sweeping the broad avenues and sedate side streets of Upper East Side Manhattan.

"I always have time for you, Margaret. What sort of delicious news do you have for me?"

Poppy was older than the Alps—old hills weren't distinguished enough to describe her—but she had never lost her taste for a juicy society scoop to fill up her "Social Scene" column.

"I thought you might have some news for me," Margaret said, and wondered if mentioning Dianne's odd behavior would stir up unwanted gossip. Poppy might share it with others, and a few wrong words from the queen of society "news" could escalate into a full-blown rumor. "Don't, please, pass on to anyone that I'm asking the questions I'm going to ask."

"Dear, dear Lady Margaret, discretion is my middle name." That was true. Poppy held many secrets in her files and in her mind that she had never made public. For Poppy, mere knowledge alone was power. "What do you want to know?"

"About the Starks," Margaret said.

"Is there a problem with Charlie and Dianne?" Poppy sounded eager.

"Not that I know of," Margaret said, "but Dianne has been in a funk, and I was wondering if you knew anything that might explain it. Of course, she has her sister here."

"Ah, yes, the one who liked Paul until she discovered he wasn't rich in his own right. Margaret, I don't trade in idle gossip. I leave that to the lunching ladies, heads together over their salads, bent on assassinating the characters of their dearest friends in the whole world. I concentrate on digging out details of massive divorce settlements, the spontaneous impregnation of otherwise virtuous women by unsuitable men, the peccadilloes of major stars and people with titles attached to them. Dianne and Charlie are nice people, who don't do that sort of thing. He's an important man, and can't afford ugly tales. A lovely man, we all adore Charlie. Dianne, of course . . ." Poppy sighed and trailed off, immediately alerting Margaret to possible revelations of some dark side of Dianne she hadn't mentioned to her best friend.

Poppy recovered. "We all adore Dianne, too, even if she does come from a different sort of world. It can't have been easy for her, stepping into Zoe Stark's shoes the way she did. Zoe was very bitter about the way Charlie shunted her aside, and she had a lot of friends and supporters in our circle. But Zoe was lucky to find that gigolo who wanted to carry her off, along with the money she got from the divorce."

Margaret did not want to hear anything about Charles Stark's former wife. The tale of her being dumped by Charlie, followed by her infatuation with a younger man deemed eminently unsuitable had been told too many times already. She'd never met Zoe Stark, but thought Zoe had displayed a certain courage and resilience in acting spontaneously to get out of her old life into a new one. "I really don't know all that much about Dianne, even though she's a good friend. She's told me about the airlines, and Karen from Rhode Island whom she thought would be perfect for Prince Paul. Her family isn't rich or social, but no scandals that I know of. And she's denied that she's involved with anyone."

"But she's not behaving quite normally." Poppy made it more of a statement than a question.

"I'm a bit worried about her is all," Margaret said. "She's been jumpy and, well, not happy. She's talking about going back to work. She feels worthless just watching the nanny care for the little boy, and working on committees that don't appreciate what she does, having her hair done, going to lunch, shopping at Ralph Lauren and Bergdorf's. The usual things. She doesn't even seem happy about having her sister to stay."

"These young women like Dianne," Poppy said wearily, "they read too much of this feminist stuff, about having it all. Well, Dianne *has* it all. Committee work is as meaningful as you make it. Raising a child is important. She has a rich husband, a nice home, decent servants. What more could she want?"

Margaret could not answer that. Dianne had a lot, everything, in fact. Except a sense of worth.

Then Poppy said, "I suppose she's told you about her admirers."

"No, Poppy. What admirers? She hasn't said a word. Who are they?" Now they were getting somewhere.

"It's nothing, really. Someone mentioned that Gerald Toth was quite attentive at the Clearys' dinner party last week, or was it the week before? Enough so that Charlie had a few words with him. And then someone told me she'd seen Dianne lunching with Antonio Palomino at Mortimer's or some such place only a few days ago. You know him of course."

"No, I do not," Margaret said.

"Just as well. He's a charmer, though. I believe he's Brazilian or maybe Cuban, but not much money. Gerald has almost Cary Grant's good looks, and he's very wealthy. He owns some sort of computer empire. I wouldn't know about computer things."

Poppy probably wouldn't. It had taken her newspaper years to convert her to a computer with a word-processing program after decades of typing her column on a rugged old standard typewriter. Computers were anathema to Poppy, who would likely still be using a quill pen dipped in ink if she weren't afraid that she would get ink spots on the lacy pink peignoir that she habitually wore in the cozy East Side apartment she rarely emerged from. But Poppy certainly kept track of the financial status of attractive new men who washed up on the beaches of New York society. And Dianne's alleged admirers sounded quite promising for her sister.

"I don't understand all this fuss about computers," Poppy said wearily, "but I do know that people can get awfully rich from them. Gerald Toth is apparently one of them. He's single and from California, and he has an eye for a pretty woman. Elinor Newhall rather took him under her wing and introduced him around. She told me he's squired about any number of lovelies since he's been in New York." It was beginning to sound even better for Karen. "I don't suppose he's settled here for good; these Californians always go home eventually, thank goodness."

"Dianne hasn't mentioned him or Antonio Palomino," Margaret said. "And she would have if they were seriously pursuing her." Actually Margaret wasn't sure anymore what Dianne would mention. "Besides, she thinks admirers are amusing, but she doesn't take them seriously. Poppy, I believe you are succumbing to the lure of idle gossip."

"You asked, and I told you what I'd heard. But mark my words, something is going on with one of them, and she's feeling guilty. Terry Thompson told me just the other day that she thought Dianne was . . . different lately."

Margaret considered her next words carefully. "So even Terry has noticed. You'll be doing Dianne a great favor if you didn't encourage that sort of talk. She's having problems, but I don't think they're romantic."

"I'd never do anything to hurt dear Dianne," Poppy said, but Margaret noticed that she sounded as though she were defending herself against an unjust accusation. What was Poppy up to?

"There's something you're not telling me," Margaret said. But Poppy chose a stubborn silence. It would take a personal plea from the Queen Mother perhaps to pry anything from Poppy when she got this way. "Oh, Poppy, how can I help her if you won't help me?"

"I have my standards, Margaret. Once I have given my word to remain silent, I keep it." Margaret imagined Poppy waving her hand toward the locked closet where she kept overflowing files of ancient secrets about simply everyone. "Listen," Poppy said, "this might explain it. I suppose you've heard that Zoe is back in New York, and she's never forgiven Dianne for capturing Charlie. I wouldn't put anything past her to get even. The romance with that fortune hunter didn't work out, after Zoe's settlement from Charlie was gone."

"Of course!" Margaret said. She could imagine Zoe making annoying phone calls, and otherwise intruding on Dianne's life. It would be enough to shake anyone.

"And," Poppy said, "you might ask Dianne about her own ex."

"Ex-husband?" Margaret was briefly shocked to learn that it was true, then went on as though she knew all about him. "Long out of the picture, according to Dianne." Why had Dianne never mentioned a prior marriage? Devious wench, and if she couldn't tell her best friend . . .

Poppy didn't appear to sense that she'd caught Margaret by surprise. "A youthful indiscretion, Dianne always calls it. Of course, one doesn't bring him up when Charlie is around. He was some high school flame from Rhode Island that she met and married before she went into the airlines. It quickly ended after she started flying off to lands grander than Providence. I've seen it happen so often. No time for the young couple to get to know each other and settle down. I think Dianne mentioned that the sister lived with them for a while, and that's always a cause for friction. The ex's never really go away though, trust me. I had the opportunity to meet him once a few years ago, just after Dianne and Charlie married. He'd seen a mention of her in my column, where I guess I used her pre-Stark name. Dianne Reid she was then. She didn't use her ex-husband's name at all, so I didn't know what he was talking about at first. He needed my help in locating her. I naturally assumed he wanted money from her, so I refused to tell him anything. Then he actually invited me to dine out with him." The horror of that possibility rang clearly through Poppy's words. She wasn't a true agoraphobic, but she certainly could count on the aged fingers of her hands the number of times she'd voluntarily set foot on the streets of New York in the years Margaret had lived in the city. "Not a bad-looking fellow, but . . . not our kind, really. Blue collar, although I understand his father was a professor of engineering at some university."

"I don't remember his name," Margaret said mendaciously, never having heard it.

Poppy said, "Harry? Larry? Barry? That's it, Barry. Calvin Barry."

Margaret pondered this unexpected but significant person from Dianne's past, and decided that Charles Stark was more than capable of handling him if he came begging. His own ex-wife was another story. If the bitterness remained, and old ties still endured, Charlie might view Zoe's position more sympathetically than Dianne would like. Margaret decided to move on to another topic.

"Tell me more about Gerald Toth." A rich and handsome computer king seemed more likely to interest Dianne than a blue-collar ex-husband, particularly if there were rough spots in her marriage. She didn't think a smooth Latin lover would appeal to the fastidious Dianne.

"Gerald is gorgeous, cultured, and *so* interesting. He's had the most amazing adventures, exploring jungles and climbing mountains, you name it." Poppy sounded a bit smitten herself. "He's taken a little place in the East Seventies, entertains some, gets invited about quite a bit, and causes many a young heart to flutter. The junior set is quite taken with him, although he must be in his forties. Leila Parkins had a fling with him, but nothing serious. That child will never settle down." Leila had been a deb

Flavor of the Season a few years back, and had never been willing to relinquish her title. She'd even captured Paul's heart for half a second. "I'm surprised you haven't encountered Gerald."

"I don't go about much anymore," Margaret said. "I have my other interests." Such as they were. As she chatted with Poppy, Margaret was beginning to feel the kind of pointlessness of life that Dianne had expressed at tea. Margaret's other interests consisted of a few courses on art history in case Kasparian needed her to help sell antiques again, and in case she ran errands for Giovanni and his decorating clients, finding fabrics and examining furniture. She'd gotten quite good at spotting fake Shaker rocking chairs. And there was Sam De Vere, when his life in the police force allowed time for her. Unless Bedros went back into business with his antiques, she had only those decorating chores for Giovanni, and the occasional charity committees that allowed her to feel somewhat good about herself. Working for world peace or raising funds to cure an awful disease had a certain appeal. "If you hear anything that might explain Dianne's lowness, please let me know. She won't talk to me, and I'm concerned."

"I'd say that Zoe was intruding, but I have no definite word about that. Nobody's really seen her at the usual places. No, wait. Somebody said she'd been spotted looking fabulous, ten years younger, a complete makeover. I guess she put some of that money she got from Charlie to good use. But you must tell *me* anything that might interest me," Poppy said. "Come around to see me one of these days, it's been far too long. Paul is coming back to town for good, I understand. I had a chat with Carolyn Sue the other day. She's actually looking forward to summer in Dallas."

Prince Paul Castrocani, fusion of rich Texas mother and impoverished aristocratic Italian father, was indeed due back from the Caribbean island of his fiancée, the Honorable Georgina Farfaine, although Margaret did not hear actual wedding bells clanging away in the near future. His occasional postcards dwelt mostly on his financial future.

"I would like to see Paul settled with a nice girl, and pretty little children. Although I imagine Carolyn Sue would not welcome the idea of being a grandmother."

"First things first," Margaret said. "He'll be looking for work, as am I. He says that United National Bank is interested in taking him on again, although I don't think he's learned much more about banking in the past couple of years than he knew when he worked for them previously."

"I'm sure he's good with customers," Poppy said. "They like a nice-looking young man to attend to them when they cash their cheques."

"Paul was not that kind of banker," Margaret said. "Not the kind who stands behind a window and cashes cheques and takes deposits. He was in international banking." But not for long, alas. He never measured up to the expectations of either his stepfather, Benton Hoopes, or his superiors at the bank.

"Oh, I know that," Poppy said. "Besides, banks now all have those machines to handle everything. You never have to speak to a living person if you don't choose to."

At least Poppy had grasped the concept of ATMs and their place in modern life.

"And what about Antonio Palomino?" Margaret asked.

"Tony is fabulous! I'm sure he's Cuban, now that I think about it. I have no idea what he does, but it may be that he smuggles cigars for a living. I keep hearing about these cigar bars around the city, where they do nothing but smoke the big ugly things, and the Cuban ones are much in demand."

"How would Dianne have met someone like him?"

"Through Charlie," Poppy said authoritatively.

"I don't believe Charlie smokes cigars," Margaret said, even though he'd gone off to the cigar bar with Karen after dinner. She preferred to think he wanted a quiet place to talk to George Armitage.

"But you never know, do you?" Poppy said darkly.

Margaret decided that Poppy had nothing further of value to offer on Dianne's situation. Except for the possibility of admirers. "The ex-husband, is he still around?"

"It was a few years ago that I encountered him. I believe he said he worked as a seaman, so he was often out of the country. That would fit, wouldn't it? I mean, if he's from Rhode Island. Rhode Island is on the water. Newport and all those lovely big houses, and the views of Narragansett Bay. I remember how wonderful it was in the old days when I was just a girl. Fabulous parties and all the best people summering there. It's still very social, but I imagine it's changed a great deal . . ." Poppy sounded wistful as she recalled the elegant Newport days and nights of her youth. "The ex-husband is probably off somewhere sailing the seas. I hardly think New York City would suit him."

"More to the point, do you know if he ever got in touch with Dianne?"

"I didn't tell him how to reach her," Poppy said. "Although it wouldn't be difficult to track the Starks down. Charlie is a pretty well-known man, and they're listed in the telephone book. I was not impressed. He was quite rude when I refused his invitation."

Margaret was uneasy. She decided that she'd have to ask Dianne directly about the surprising ex-husband.

Chapter 4

The windows of the Starks' living room looked down on Fifth Avenue and its flowing stream of headlights headed downtown, with a glimpse of Central Park, a dark pool of trees backed by gleams of light from the buildings across the park. Dianne cautiously drew back the edge of the curtain so she could survey the sidewalk and the avenue without being visible to anyone looking up at the windows. A few pedestrians hurried along past the building, but she was too high up to see if anyone was loitering nearby or across the street along the edge of the park. In any case, a loiterer could be around the corner near the entrance canopy but concealed by parked cars to escape the notice of the doorman.

At least she had no social obligations to take her out tonight, so she was safe in the apartment until morning. Charlie had called to say he was dining with colleagues from work, but would not be late. She was convinced he was dining with his former wife, Zoe, who was having some sort of crisis and needed his advice. Dianne didn't worry much about Zoe. Her sister Karen said she was going to a Broadway show with an old college classmate now living in New York, but for all Dianne knew, she could be the one dining with Charlie, who seemed to find her bawdy tongue and naked lust after the good things of life amusing.

Chip was asleep in his crib, and Lourdes had retired to her room. Dianne could never imagine what the patient, mostly humorless Filipina woman gained from watching hours of American sitcoms.

Dianne took one last look down at Fifth Avenue, and a figure on the sidewalk across the street caught her eye. Someone—a man, she thought—had stepped into the glow from a streetlight and was looking up at her building. He was too far away for her to identify, and there was nothing about him to indicate that he was looking up specifically at her windows. She let the curtain drop. Fortunately the room was dark, so even if he had been focusing on the Stark apartment, he could not have seen her.

"You're crazy," she said aloud to herself, and left the window, turning down the hall to reach her bedroom. She could hear the faint sound of canned laughter from the nanny's room off the kitchen. She hoped that Lourdes would not decide that Lucy Ricardo was a role model to emulate. Slapstick physical comedy in these surroundings would not please Charlie, even if she was the perfect nanny. She was definitely not a madcap, and she worshiped little Chip, and would never allow harm to befall him.

Dianne paused in the middle of the darkened bedroom. She'd already gone over and over a scenario where someone approached Lourdes while she was wheeling Chip in his stroller along the edge of the park, and it frightened her to think of it. Then she relaxed. Lourdes would fight like a demon to protect him. Dianne didn't even like to think the word kidnapper. But the park was relatively safe where the other nannies and their charges gathered, even though Lourdes was not comfortable with the snooty English nannies so many of the parents in this neighborhood were hiring. Nor did she approve of the slim, blond Scandinavian au pairs, or the sleek French girls, or even the Latinas who minded children while their mothers were doing "important things," like taking tea at fashionable hotels or having their hair done by a petulant and high-priced hairdresser.

She ran her fingers through her new, slightly reddish hair. She'd always been a blonde, and decided she wanted to be one again. Tomorrow, if she could arrange an appointment. Karen was probably thinking she'd mimic Dianne's new reddish rinse. It would serve her right if Dianne changed back just after Karen had made the plunge into henna.

Dianne slipped over to the window that faced on the side street, where the entrance to the building was located. She could see the edge of the canopy, but there was no one about, not even people walking their dogs, or doormen from neighboring buildings outside on the quiet street smoking cigarettes. Then she spotted someone carrying a large white cone of paper topped with greenery and a flash of color. A florist's deliveryman. From her perspective she couldn't see where he went. She moved away from the window and started to change into a silk paisley caftan to await Charlie's return.

She barely heard the discreet ring of the house phone down the hallway, but she was briefly alarmed. Then she shook it off and answered the phone. It was the doorman.

"Flower delivery, Mrs. Stark. Should I send it up with one of the boys? I know you said no deliveries, but the guy said it was real important that you get the flowers so they won't die."

"My husband will be home soon, or my sister," she said. "No, have someone bring it up. They may be very late." Karen could easily be swayed by anybody into making a long night of it, and if Zoe's crisis was monumental, Charlie, too, could be late.

She decided that the sexy caftan was not appropriate wear for opening the door to one of the building's staff, so she slipped on the pinkish trench coat she kept in the hall closet for spring wear and waited for the bell. The top drawer of the small table in the hall held a handful of dollar bills for emergency tips, so she was ready when the bell rang.

Miguel, the slight Puerto Rican who was one of the building's handymen, was almost hidden by the huge bouquet. It looked like the same white cone she had seen being delivered earlier. "Señora, she is beautiful flowers."

"Indeed they are," Dianne said, and took the bundle, slipping a couple of dollars into his hand. "Thank you so much, Miguel." She supposed the flowers were from Charlie, a sort of apology for entertaining Zoe and leaving her alone. It was nice to know that he still liked to surprise her.

She closed the door and carried the flowers to her little arranging room off the kitchen. The small, sharp knife she used for trimming stems was on the counter. Stripping away the paper, she found a mass of fragrant lilies, as well as roses, carnations, daisies, sweet peas, with some baby's breath and greens. Then she gasped. Mixed in with the live flowers were clumps of dead blooms, ugly dried flowers, emitting a subtle, nauseating stench. She dropped the bouquet, then looked for the envelope, knowing Charlie would never have sent her such a gift.

There was only a florist's tag from La Vie en Rose,

with her name, address, and apartment number stapled to the outside wrapping paper. She had already gotten out a wide-mouthed vase, filled it with water, and taken out the little knife for cutting the stems before she saw the horrible additions to the bouquet. Now she dumped the whole mess into the trash. Then she saw the card, a small white envelope tucked in among the flowers in the wastepaper basket.

You know I care, the message said. *And I know you care, too, but we must meet again.* There was no name, only a squiggle that might be a "G" or a "C."

Surely Gerald Toth was not going to pursue her after that bit of flirtation at the Clearys'. And it wasn't his style at all to send a gift like this. Instead of trash flowers, he'd be more likely to send a van of orchids or a diamond bracelet. But she was kidding herself. She didn't want it to be either a "G" or a "C."

She didn't need this. Nothing in her short acquaintance with Gerald had given any indication that she "cared" for him other than as a pleasant and casual friend, and she'd done nothing to inspire this mean gesture. Carefully she put the trimming knife away in a drawer, and pulling the trench coat tightly around her, left the room. She carried the card with her and put it in the drawer of the night table on her side of the bed, crawled under the sheets, and pulled the blanket over her head. She wouldn't wait up for Charlie and Karen. No face cream tonight, no careful removal of makeup and hot bath.

Gone was the hope for some sisterly conversation over a late-night cup of hot chocolate, the way they used to before Karen's envy damaged their relationship all those years ago. It had started because she'd gotten married first, was the first to leave home, the first to have a glamorous job—even though she'd argued that working for the airlines was tiring and difficult—the first to be lucky enough to marry a millionaire. Well, that didn't happen to everybody, and it, too, could be tiring and difficult, with a number of hidden dangers.

She was tempted to confide her fears to Margaret, who was entirely sensible, but even so, Margaret would probably think she was crazy. Karen also wouldn't take this other business seriously, the fact that someone was watching her all the time. Whenever she went out, she saw him in the shadows, and she knew she wasn't just imagining it. She'd tried to tell Charlie, who was convinced she was imagining things, but she wasn't. He was there. Karen wouldn't even believe the threatening letter she'd gotten the morning of the day she'd had tea with Margaret at Villa d'Este. Karen had always been less serious than Dianne, but people always knew immediately that they were sisters. However, she'd been a comfort when Dianne's marriage with Cal had broken down, even though Dianne knew there had once been something between them. Calvin was incorrigible.

I'll find Karen a husband, Dianne thought, one as good as Charlie, much better than Calvin Barry. Prince Paul wasn't married yet, so there was still hope for a title for her little sister. If only Gerald would rise to the bait. If he liked Dianne, he'd certainly like Karen, much more of a free spirit. And, besides, she could talk reasonably intelligently about computers, which Dianne couldn't.

As she tried to sleep, a terrible suspicion began to take shape. It was something she'd known all along, but refused to admit. It wasn't Charlie, it wasn't Gerald. It wasn't even Zoe, but she knew who it must be. Calvin Barry. The man she hadn't seen for more than half a decade had come back to haunt her. What could he want, and why was he doing this to her? When they divorced, he'd said he'd never loved her, but one of her girlfriends said that all men say that to justify parting from their wives. But why did he think she still cared? Why did the note say that he still cared for her? The silent phone calls, the stalking, the strange letter that had threatened her—she had thought they were jokes in poor taste. Or maybe the reaction of that building porter she'd complained about and who had then been fired. Or even Gerald's way of responding to her rejection of his invitation to greater intimacy. She tried to be careful, hoping that it would all just go away, but taking care did not seem to solve anything.

Dianne Stark was suddenly frightened. Her careful life was slowly being bent out of shape.

She would have to tell someone.

Chapter 5

"*Dianne Stark* won't be able to attend the committee meeting," Margaret told Elinor Newhall over the phone the next morning, and was rewarded with a sniff of disgust. "She promised to call you, but she's been terribly busy. Her sister is visiting."

"She hasn't called, and she's been to only one meeting in two months," Elinor said. "If you're going to make a commitment to an important affair like ours, you simply have to live up to your promises. She could just bring along her sister to help. Although Emily Armitage reports that the sister was making quite a play for Charlie the other night. And even George, to hear Emily tell it. Maybe she's not our sort. Emily doesn't think much of her."

"I'll be there," Margaret said quickly. It did not seem wise to be on Elinor's bad side, especially since Margaret had arranged for her to interview Giovanni about redecorating her sprawling summer home in the Hamptons at an enormous price. It would mean a welcome and large commission for Margaret. It wouldn't happen this year, of course. It was too near the summer season to start such a major project. Margaret understood that Elinor planned to rent out the house this year for a huge monthly sum, allow the renters to wreak their havoc, then charge them for damages and use those funds and the rent to help pay for a fall redecoration. The wealthy do not stay rich by failing to figure all the angles.

"I know I can always count on you, Margaret. Dianne is another story. She's a lovely girl, but she doesn't have Zoe's character, which is good and solid in spite of her infatuation with that dreadful man after Charlie abandoned her. Did you hear, by the way, that Zoe's back in New York? Dianne has been a bit odd lately. Probably because of Zoe."

"Odd?" Someone else had noticed.

"Short-tempered. Nervous. Although, Lord knows, I'd be rattled to bits by having a baby at home all the time and an ex-wife on my doorstep."

"She has a nanny," Margaret said. "I don't think little Chipper upsets her life at all. And I don't believe Zoe has been bothering her."

"Something's upset her. Or someone." Elinor lowered her voice. "I suppose you heard the talk about her and Gerald Toth, and then there's that . . . that . . . Argentine fellow."

"I thought he was Cuban," Margaret said.

"Then you *have* heard! I was almost afraid to mention it, since you and Dianne are such good friends. What does she have to say?"

"She hasn't mentioned a word about either of them."

"I understand," Elinor said. "You don't want to gossip. Very laudable. And loyal."

"No, really. She hasn't spoken of either of them. I just heard something from Poppy."

"Gerald was around for drinks a few nights ago, and he

went on and on about Dianne. I think he's quite smitten. Dianne could do worse. He's gorgeous and very rich."

"I don't think Dianne is looking for anyone other than Charlie," Margaret said, with no hope that her words would deflect Elinor.

"You know how things work," Elinor said. "I really would like to know what's going on with her and Gerald."

Aha! thought Margaret. I certainly do know how things work. Elinor herself is casting a lustful eye on Gerald Toth. She recalled that Elinor had a rather colorful past that included involvement with other women's husbands as well as the occasional unencumbered male. Karen Reid might be the perfect buddy for Elinor.

"As far as I know, things are not going on at all. Although I agree that Dianne hasn't been herself lately. I'd like to meet this gorgeous Mr. Toth."

"Of course! I'll give a little dinner . . ." She hesitated then. Perhaps she was worried that Margaret would fascinate him and cut Elinor out, but Elinor was a brave woman. "I'm having people over this evening, just for drinks, and Gerald has promised to join us. Seven-thirtyish? I know it's short notice, but it's nothing fancy. My husband plays poker on Wednesdays, so I entertain informally when he's out."

After the call Margaret pondered Elinor Newhall. Forty or so, not unattractive, known for dressing very well. Twice married, now to an ordinary but prosperous poker-playing businessman. A couple of children gone from home, a lot of committee work. Somewhat dictatorial, but that comes with chairlady territory. And perhaps a woman who coveted—what had Poppy said?—a man with Cary Grant good looks, who would satisfy her desire for clandestine meetings and a few pretty gifts. Nothing serious, probably. In spite of her past achievements, Elinor was surely not one to inspire raving lust in a man who, from all reports, should have a pack of women falling at his feet. In Margaret's opinion, Elinor would not be such a man's first choice, but it could be fun for Elinor to have someone to give her empty life a bit of substance. That being the case, Karen would not be welcome.

Something worthwhile. Margaret wondered again if Dianne had even for a moment thought of Gerald Toth in those terms. She decided that she would ask Dianne herself. Then she concluded that, despite Elinor, it was a brilliant idea to fix Karen up with Gerald Toth.

The phone rang several times, but it was not a machine that finally answered.

"Mrs. Stark is not in." It must be the nanny who answered. Margaret detected an unfamiliar accent.

"Would you tell her please that her friend Margaret Priam wishes her to return the call? Thank you so much." Margaret heard a clunk as the receiver was placed roughly on wood, then after a moment Dianne was on the line.

"Margaret, is that really you?" She sounded trembly.

"And who else would it be, using my name?"

"I don't know. So many weird things have been happening lately. Someone sending me dead flowers, and horrible letters. People calling and hanging up before the machine even starts, or else saying they're somebody I know well, and then it turns out to be . . ." Dianne stopped speaking, and Margaret waited.

"Turns out to be who, exactly?"

"Nothing. I'm just being silly. That's why I usually don't allow Lourdes to answer the phone. I guess she forgot this time."

"Is someone seriously harassing you, Dianne?" Margaret did not like the sound of all this.

"Not really." Dianne didn't sound convincing. "It's just somebody's idea of a joke." Then Margaret heard her say away from the receiver, "It's all right, Lourdes. It really is Lady Margaret."

"Dianne," Margaret said firmly. "I know something is going on. Please tell me. If there's trouble, you know I'll help, and so will De Vere."

"No trouble, honestly. I don't want to involve the police. Charlie would hate that. And I'd have to tell him . . ."

Margaret didn't want to think about what she'd have to tell Charlie. "Look, are you at home for the next couple of hours?"

"I don't go out much, even when Charlie arranges the car. I'm alone today. Karen has gone shopping, and that will take hours."

"I'll be there in half an hour, and you're going to explain a few things." Dianne did not protest.

It took Margaret rather longer than expected to walk over the few blocks from her high-rise apartment building to Fifth and then down a couple blocks to the Starks' street. The spring afternoon was so pleasant that she couldn't bring herself to rush, so she loitered in front of shopwindows full of things she had no desire to buy, and even stopped to read the menu in the window of a new Italian restaurant that promised to open soon.

This was New York at its best, as far as she was concerned. Mothers with strollers full of happy babies, scruffy college students tossing Frisbees across Lexington Avenue despite the traffic, and at the end of the cross streets, glimpses of Central Park, trees already green. The apartment buildings had blooming flower boxes on the windowsills, and the doormen lounged under their canopies, enjoying the afternoon sun. How often in past years had the seasons in New York slipped from winter to summer with barely a glance at spring, with cold and rainy days abruptly becoming hot and humid, full summer, in fact, almost overnight. But this year, spring was unfolding gracefully, with fresh mild air and pale blue skies.

Although her spirits were buoyed by the day, Margaret was never forgetful of her nagging concern about Dianne. She reviewed the possibilities: Charlie was not young, so his health might be worrying his younger wife. Then there were Dianne's cryptic comments. She didn't want police help, she had stopped going out much, she seemed to be expecting to see someone around every corner, and she was nervous and fretful. She was feeling worthless. She wanted to get away, to go back to work. She certainly behaved oddly in the matter of telephone calls. Margaret kept coming back to the possibility of a romance with the much-publicized Gerald Toth or even the mysterious Latin, Antonio Palomino. It could be that Dianne's admirer was becoming too forward and making the possible relationship too obvious to poor Charlie, whom Dianne would surely not wish to hurt. That alone would be enough to put her in an unsteady mood.

For a moment she wondered if the ex-husband was intruding into her life, or even Charlie's ex-wife. She felt a twinge of guilt. Surely Zoe had not become a raving lunatic after all this time, but there was no reason to dismiss the ex-husband; he was far more likely to be hovering in the shadows, waiting to do . . . what? Reclaim Dianne? Ask for money? Get even? That was silly. She had no idea why they had parted and divorced. If the husband had left Dianne, there should be no question of "getting even." She ought to ask Dianne straight out about the circumstances of the divorce. If she would be willing to tell her best friend.

Margaret turned off Lexington onto the Starks' cross street, and proceeded toward Park Avenue. She paused on the corner of Park to admire a massive steel statue that had been placed temporarily on the meridian strip between the uptown and downtown lanes.

She crossed with the light and continued on toward Madison. At the northwest corner of Madison, a homeless man sat in the shade of a building with an empty cardboard coffee container in his outstretched hand to capture the largesse of passing strangers. He was quite young and fair-haired, with a full bushy beard and surprisingly intelligent eyes. She'd seen him before on this corner or one nearby when she was walking to the Starks' building. New York was full of beggars, whom one saw at their regular posts.

"Thank you, ma'am," he said politely when she dropped a quarter into his cup. "You have a nice day, now."

"I hope I will," Margaret said. "And the same to you."

"Not many real nice days for my kind, ma'am, but I get along okay. At least the weather's good." He had a neat backpack on the ground beside him, and while his jeans and T-shirt were not spotless, he looked fairly well maintained.

Margaret continued on, having not much else to discuss with the homeless man. Three quarters of the way down the block, she reached Dianne's building.

"Lady Margaret for Mrs. Stark," she said as she entered and breezed past the doorman and headed for the elevator.

"Hold on," the doorman said. "I have to ring upstairs for all visitors. Mrs. Stark's orders."

Margaret halted, puzzled. He must know her, she'd been there often enough, and she remembered they'd once discussed the fact that she was English, because he'd noticed her accent. And she'd noticed his. He claimed to be Yugoslavian. In any event, the formality of announcing her impending arrival had never been an issue.

"Orders just for me?" she asked.

"Everybody. Just got the word. No one is allowed up to the Starks unless I call first. Even if you was her mother." He shrugged. "The tenants are the boss. They can get you fired if you don't follow orders. Reuben got canned last week because he did something Mrs. Stark didn't like. And was he mad."

Someone answered the house phone, because he gave Margaret's name and then nodded in the direction of the elevator.

"Have the Starks been having trouble with unwelcome visitors?" she asked.

The doorman shrugged again. "Not that I know of. I just got my orders." He jerked his chin toward the elevators. "She's expecting you."

Margaret entered the mirrored elevator, and the doors closed silently. The cab moved upward with the utmost refinement, quite unlike the lurches of the faux wood-paneled elevator in her own otherwise very nice, recently built apartment building. The difference, she decided, between old money buildings and nouveau construction lies in the degree of comfort in vertical transportation. This elevator even had a thick plush carpet on the floor.

A plump Filipina woman answered her ring. Lourdes.

Margaret remembered her. She had enviably thick, glossy black hair, and a shy smile.

"Mrs. Stark is in the living room," Lourdes said. "The housekeeper is out, and the sister is out as well, so I am making lemonade. The little boy is napping."

"I know the way," Margaret said. "Wait," she added as Lourdes started away toward the kitchen. The nanny turned back.

"Has Mrs. Stark been unwell? I mean, I've noticed that she hasn't looked quite right lately, nervous and tired."

Lourdes's expression told her nothing. "She is very well. Maybe a little tired. She does not sleep well. I hear her walking about the apartment at night." Then, almost flustered, Lourdes half whispered, "She does not always sleep in the room with Mr. Stark. She says it is because her wakefulness disturbs him. Sometimes she sleeps on the daybed in the room with the baby, or in one of the guest bedrooms, and since that sister is visiting, she sometimes even sleeps on the sofa in the drawing room." Lourdes's expression said eloquently that this was not proper behavior for a dutiful wife. "She is waiting for you." Lourdes's tone of voice indicated that she was not willing to discuss her employer further, and that Margaret should get moving and let her make the lemonade.

Margaret went into the big living room. If Dianne had arranged the flowers, she had done a grand job. The room was a comfortable mix of traditional and modern furnishings, and the colors were beige, brown, and black, so that the vases of yellow and orange tulips seemed to bring sunlight into the place. Dianne herself was standing at the window, peering out from behind the curtain at the street below.

"Hullo, it's me," Margaret said.

"Yes. I thought you'd be here sooner. Lourdes is bringing us lemonade. I thought that would be nice for a spring afternoon, and maybe some cookies. The housekeeper is always making cookies. I suppose it makes her feel busy when there's not much else to do, although Karen seems to take great pleasure in issuing orders to the servants. But they're lovely cookies: meringues and lemon bars and things sprinkled with poppy seeds. Or if you'd prefer, we could have a Campari. Or Lourdes could bring us some lunch. She makes wonderful club sandwiches. I practically live on them nowadays. But I have her make them with low-fat mayonnaise, so it's okay." Dianne was as slim as a birch tree.

"Lemonade is fine for me," Margaret said, but Dianne scarcely noticed her reply and continued to chatter and peek out the window through a little space between the curtain and the wall.

"I love watching the traffic on Fifth, the horse-drawn carriages full of tourists, and the buses and the limos. You can see the seasons change just by watching the trees in the park." Margaret couldn't help but notice the white knuckles as Dianne grasped the edge of the curtain.

"Please, Dianne, stop, sit, stay. And please, please tell me what's worrying you."

Dianne came away from the windows and sank into a big cozy armchair upholstered in heavy beige duck cloth. She looked even more haggard than when Margaret had seen her at the Villa d'Este. Margaret sat across from her on a sofa, and as she did, she could see two tears gather at the corners of Dianne's eyes and then slowly move down her cheeks.

"Darling, please. Let me help," Margaret said.

Dianne put her hands to her face. "Oh, Margaret. I can't involve you."

"You can. Just tell me."

"I'm afraid," Dianne said. "I'm afraid someone is going to kill me."

Chapter 6

"*Ridiculous!*" Margaret said. "You're imagining things."

"I knew you wouldn't believe me, but it's true. And if they don't kill me, I'm afraid for Charlie and Chip. Lourdes, even." Dianne kept her hands to her face, and Margaret could see her shoulders shaking.

It was time to be businesslike, since Dianne had clearly lost control.

"You have to explain why you think someone's going to kill you, and then we'll decide what to do about it."

Dianne stood up and left the room briefly. When she returned, she handed Margaret a grubby business-size envelope with her name and address written out in a somewhat childish hand. "Go on, read it," she said.

Margaret took out the single sheet, and her eyes widened as she read quickly. The writer stated clearly that he—Margaret assumed that it was a man—"would see Dianne dead" if she did not agree to see him. "After all we have been to each other, you can't just cut me off. I will see that you and yours suffer for treating me this way."

Margaret looked up at Dianne. "Who sent this? Have you called the police? I told you Sam would help. Shall I call him now?"

"You have to swear you believe me. Charlie doesn't believe me about someone watching me all the time, always outside the door. He says I'm imagining things."

"But you showed him this letter, didn't you?"

Dianne shook her head. "Not yet, but it will only upset him. Besides, he scarcely speaks to me these days, although he has plenty to say to Karen. I . . . we don't even sleep in the same room most nights. I'm having trouble sleeping, and when I try to read, the light bothers him. And now Lourdes doesn't understand why I decided she can't take the baby to the park without one of the handymen from the building or me trailing after her. I'm afraid she'll quit and go home to Manila."

"I'm waiting to hear who is doing this," Margaret said. "Is it the man you got fired? Reuben?"

Dianne shook her head and sat quietly, apparently gathering her wits and courage to explain. "It was a misunderstanding with Reuben. He didn't stay close to Lourdes and Chip when he was supposed to. I . . . I was so upset, I acted without thinking, but of course I couldn't explain. Besides, Charlie got him another job, and he's perfectly happy with it." Before she had a chance to say more, however, the nanny bustled in with a silver tray loaded with frosty glasses, a pitcher of lemonade, and a plate of cookies. Lourdes had a youthful face, although Margaret was sure Dianne had said she was a mature woman, in her forties, with plenty of experience in caring for small children. Margaret noticed that while she smiled broadly, she cast a worried look at Dianne before setting down the tray. Then she hovered at the doorway.

"You didn't eat today," Lourdes said. "The housekeeper said you didn't even take breakfast. Can I make you a club sandwich?"

"No. I'm not hungry. You can go, Lourdes," Dianne said. "We don't need anything else."

"Ah . . . Mrs. Stark, a letter came for you."

Margaret heard Dianne's sharp intake of breath. "Letter? Who is it from? Who brought it?"

"Someone left an envelope at the doorman's desk. It had your name on it, so he gave it to me when I came back from the walk with Chipper." Dianne looked up. "Edgardo went to the park with us, just like you said. The doorman didn't see who left it. He said he was in the package room at the time."

"Where is it?" Dianne sounded shrill. Lourdes took a square white envelope from her apron pocket and handed it to Dianne, who clutched it but did not open it. She was breathing heavily. "Okay, Lourdes. That will be all."

Lourdes backed away out of the room, but she was frowning. Dianne slumped back in her chair, still holding onto the envelope.

"All right, my friend," Margaret said. "What's this all about?"

"I don't know," Dianne said. She looked at the envelope. "It's not the same handwriting as the other letter. It could just be an invitation. You know how these women think that hand-delivered invitations are like something out of a damned fairy tale. 'Her Highness requests your presence at her ball, and please wear your glass slippers in case Prince Charming shows up.' "

"You won't know unless you open it," Margaret said sensibly. "It looks like a greeting card to me. Is it your birthday?" Margaret suddenly realized that she didn't even know when Dianne's birthday was.

Dianne shook her head. "Not until September. But it was this week, years ago . . ." She stopped, but continued to stare at the envelope. Margaret waited. Dianne was so obviously disturbed that she didn't want to nag; but if something sinister was really going on, matters had to be cleared up promptly. Margaret got up, poured a glass of lemonade, and took a couple of cookies to kill time until Dianne decided to speak.

Maybe, Margaret was thinking, it was a message from one of her "admirers," and not another threat.

"Aren't you going to open it?" she asked. "And then you can explain what the problem is."

Dianne hesitated, then slit the flap. Margaret could see that it was some sort of greeting card, with a flower design on the front. Dianne opened it cautiously, and closed it immediately. She crumpled the card and the envelope, and tossed them away angrily. "It's nothing," she said. "A joke. An unpleasant joke." Her hand was trembling. "I really can't explain to you. I'm sorry I made you come all this way, just to hear me talk like a demented person. I must be hallucinating. The doctor gave me some medication for my nerves and to help me sleep, and it's just made me worse."

"Dianne, I've seen one seriously threatening letter, and I do believe that it's more than a joke. Let me help."

"If only I had something worthwhile to do with my life. A place to go every day with a task to accomplish." Then she said sadly, "But that's impossible. I don't like to leave the apartment. I can't." For a moment she brightened. "Maybe I'm catching the Poppy Dill disease, only worse. I'm trapped in this place by a silly fear that someone's waiting for me outdoors."

"Your life is very worthwhile," Margaret said. "Little Chip and Charlie depend on you to make a nice home, and I don't care how many servants and nannies you have.

Charlie and Chip don't love them. They love you. They need you."

"You're right," Dianne said, "but what good will I be if I'm dead?" She stood up. "Thank you for being here to listen to my craziness. Now, I really should start dressing. Charlie and I are invited for cocktails at the Chamberlains' this evening. Quite early, and then Charlie promised to take me to a restaurant in the Village, where we know nobody and nobody knows us. Indian or Thai, something like that. And we can walk around and look at the shopwindows, places where they have all those exotic little trinkets. I suppose my sister will want to come with us. There's nobody who likes to look at stuff more than she does."

"I'd like to see Karen," Margaret said. To herself she said, And ask her what she's up to, not that it would do any good. Karen seemed to march to her own drummer.

"She should be home anytime now, if you'd care to wait. She can't spend all of Charlie's money today."

"I have things to do myself, but I hope we'll have a chance to get together." All right, if Dianne wasn't going to open up about the ex, it wasn't Margaret's place to press her. "I want you to promise that you will call the police about that letter," she said, but Dianne wouldn't meet her eyes. "I think you know who is bothering you, and I won't leave without asking one thing that you might find an invasion of privacy. It's something Poppy mentioned. She wasn't gossiping, that's not her way, but she mentioned Gerald Toth and Antonio Palomino . . . in relation to you."

The names didn't appear to cause any reaction in Dianne. "Gerald is quite the swell" is all she said, "and Tony is a charmer. But they have nothing to do with me. I have to admit that at first I thought Gerald might be playing a joke, or Zoe, but that's impossible. If people are talking about me and Gerald, one of the lunching ladies probably imagined that Gerry or Tony or both became infatuated with my stunning beauty and wit. Maybe Elinor is acting out her jealousy by spreading rumors about me and possible liaisons. I've lunched with Tony, and Gerry has paid court at parties, but between you and me, they're chiefly interested in what Charlie can do for them. And Gerald is already so rich, even Charlie can't do much for him. Absolute truth, Margaret. I do not have a lover. I don't even have an idle romance going." She was heading for the door. "After all this time, you can find your way out, if you don't mind. I've got to do something with my hair. I'm going back to blond. If you don't look perfect, you know how they talk."

"What about . . ." Margaret was on the brink of asking about the ex-husband, but Dianne was gone.

Margaret, without shame, fumbled about, taking another cookie or two. She dropped one on the nice beige carpet, in case Dianne returned. When she stooped to recover it, she also picked up the crumpled greeting card and stuffed it into her pocket. In any case, Dianne wasn't there to notice. Margaret departed the living room and glimpsed Dianne at the end of the hall entering a bedroom.

"I'll see you soon, darling," Margaret called. "Or I'll ring you after the committee meeting."

Dianne turned back and came with her to the apartment door. "I'm sorry I'm being so silly. Forgive me. One day I'll explain."

An air kiss at the door, and Margaret departed, feeling that Dianne had recovered her equilibrium for the moment, although she had not explained fully what was troubling her, and the problem had not been solved. The threatening letter answered a lot of questions about her nervousness, but how serious was it? De Vere had always told her that he viewed any threat as serious, and this one appeared to have a certain emotional content to it.

As the elevator moved ponderously downward, Margaret took the wadded-up greeting card from her pocket and smoothed it out. The light in the elevator was surprisingly faint for such an expensive address, but she could see the word "Greetings" in script across the top of the card above the bouquet of flowers. When she reached the ground floor and stepped out into the lobby, she opened the card. "Happy anniversary to my beautiful wife," the type read. "I'll always love you." There was a scrawled message and a signature written in ballpoint. It looked like a "C." Margaret sighed. It certainly wasn't Charlie. Poppy had been somewhat vague about the name of the man Dianne had once been married to, but Margaret seemed to recall it was Calvin. Had they married in the spring about this time, many years ago perhaps? If so, it was certainly in bad taste to send an anniversary card to a long-divorced and now happily remarried woman. But at least he'd remembered the anniversary, even if Dianne judged it to be an unpleasant joke. She looked at the almost illegible message, and made out, "Seeing you again was great. You know I'll do anything for you."

The thought that Dianne had actually agreed to see Cal was certainly unpleasant to contemplate. In her own case, it had taken Margaret several years to be willing to reestablish communications again with her own long-divorced husband, and even now when she saw him on her occasional visits to England, conversation was awkward, although she felt no ill will. At least he was content in his present life, and had no reason or desire to contact her out of the blue, but that chapter of her life was effectively closed, and she'd never dream of reopening it. She thought her former husband felt exactly the same way. But maybe the same could not be said of Dianne's former husband. Poppy had suggested that the ex-husband had tried to learn Dianne's whereabouts from her. Margaret had certainly heard of former husbands who, feeling the pinch of poverty, had approached their ex-wives in the hope of sharing in the ladies' good fortune acquired by virtue of a new marriage. Charlie Stark was someone who had wealth to spare, and if the ex-husband had done his research, he would know that. But if the ex was threatening Dianne, how could he expect to reap any benefit from her present status? Why would he want to kill her? Harm Charlie or the baby? That was no way to wangle a stipend from the ample Stark fortune. But if Dianne had actually met with him, maybe she had convinced him of his folly. Or increased his determination.

She stopped at the doorman's side. "Excuse me. I wonder if you could give me some information about Mrs. Stark."

The man turned to her sharply. It was not the same man who had been on duty when she arrived. "No information about the Starks. Nothing. You'd better run along, lady, or I'll call security."

"But you know me. José, isn't it? Lady Margaret Priam. I visit Mrs. Stark frequently. You yourself have announced me any number of times."

"I have my instructions, ma'am. No questions, no answers. Mrs. Stark is very firm about it. No discussion of her, no gifts, no letters."

"I see," Margaret said. "So someone has been sending her things. Like the card for her that was given to Lourdes to bring to her."

"I was only away from the desk for a minute. There was a delivery for someone that I had to put in the package room. I never saw the guy, he just left it here and ran." The doorman sounded defensive.

"Ran? So you saw him?"

"Not even a quick look. I saw somebody out on the street, but I don't know if it was the same person who left the letter. I've seen him around the neighborhood, though, but he's never come into this building. Ordinary guy, jeans and shades, running shoes. He looked like most young guys do nowadays. Come to think of it, maybe I seen Mrs. Stark talking to him just yesterday." Margaret was attentive, but he finally shook his head. "Naw, it was probably some other lady from the building. He was just begging."

"Oh, you mean the fellow who sits on the corner of Madison. The one with the beard."

"John? No way. He's been around for months. Doesn't really panhandle, either, just sits there with his old coffee cup in case somebody drops in some change. John's okay. There was a guy who brought the flowers for Mrs. Stark the other day, but he was the real deliveryman from the florist over on Madison. Him I know from other times. I guess I shouldn't have sent them up to her, after they said she didn't want to receive anything from anybody, but the delivery guy begged me, very expensive, he said they were, and he'd catch hell if he didn't deliver them.

What could I do? And when I called up to the apartment, she said to have one of the boys bring them up." He shrugged. "This job will give you ulcers if it don't kill you first."

Margaret agreed that he could have done nothing other than what he'd done: See that the flowers were delivered. But she shuddered inwardly. Poor Dianne. How awful to have someone pursuing you with gifts and messages, and telephone calls.

Once again, she considered the possibilities. Dianne led a pretty open life, so other than the ex-husband she'd never mentioned, she surely couldn't have a closet full of dark secrets and obsessed admirers.

Admirers. Margaret imagined that while men like computer millionaire Gerald Toth and macho Latino Antonio Palomino were accustomed to having their way—and might as easily pester Dianne as a long-unseen ex—they were men of the world with better ways to approach her and win her attention. On the other hand, an obsession was an obsession, and it didn't matter much if you were the king of the universe or a sailor home from the sea. She was betting on the ex-husband.

But why was Dianne reluctant to confide in her? Together they could put a stop to this, with Sam De Vere's help and the help of the New York Police. They probably wouldn't even have to bring Charlie into it. She'd ask Sam what to do, in spite of Dianne. Then she had a brilliant idea. Sister Karen. Surely she would know what the former husband was like, whether he was likely to undertake an unpleasant stalking of Dianne. She'd even know whether the divorce was amicable and whether he left it claiming to love Dianne still. And she'd know when Dianne had gotten married, which would tie in the anniversary card and the ex.

Even if Dianne wouldn't confide in Margaret, she'd probably confided in Karen a lot over the years.

Chapter 7

*M*argaret resolutely headed toward her apartment on foot, determined to find De Vere as soon as possible. Halfway down the block, she caught a glimpse of a man in jeans and sneakers, wearing shades, who was busy lighting a cigarette in the shadow of a doorway across the street. He moved away back toward Fifth as a taxi careened down the street and halted in front of the Starks' building. Margaret didn't pay much attention and continued on toward Madison.

She scarcely acknowledged the greeting of her new friend, the homeless man on the corner of Madison, because she was engrossed in thinking about obsessions. She was definitely looking forward to meeting Gerald Toth at Elinor's cocktail party. Then she was sorry she hadn't persuaded Elinor to invite Antonio as well. All the suspects together over the vichyssoise.

Suspects in what? She didn't even know what the problem was exactly, except for a vaguely written death threat.

Margaret, she told herself firmly, a death threat is sufficient, vague or not. She was determined to put a stop to this nonsense.

The loud noise nearly a block behind her caused her to

stop and look back. The homeless man had gotten to his feet and was looking in the same direction.

There was a sudden flurry of activity outside the building. Several people were gathered around a heap of something on the ground. Margaret started to run back. She was sure it was a person lying there. Then she heard the ambulance sirens and police sirens. The homeless man jogged along with her, but before they could reach the spot, two, then three police cars had converged on the street outside the apartment building, and an ambulance arrived.

"Oh, jeez, somebody got shot," the homeless man said. "You heard it, didn't you?"

"I heard something," Margaret said. They were almost at the building. The men from the ambulance were working on the body lying on the ground. Margaret thought she could see blood. Then the EMS crew were placing the person on a stretcher and loading it into the back of the ambulance. Uniformed policemen were putting up tape to protect the site while two or three raced down the street toward Central Park.

"What happened?" Margaret asked the doorman, who was looking pale and wiping his brow.

"I dunno. I was standing inside there by the desk, and this cab pulls up. Lady gets out with a whole lot of shopping bags, so I go out to help her. It's Mrs. Stark's sister who's visiting her. Looks a lot like her. Then some guy just walks up to her when I'm starting to go into the building with the bags. The next thing I hear is a shot, and she's lying on the ground and I see blood, and the guy's taking off toward Central Park. So I call 911 fast, and cops and the EMS guys get here. I told 'em what I saw, and a bunch of them went running to the park. And then I had to call up to Mrs. Stark. I told the Filipina lady what had happened, and she started crying and screaming. There's Mrs. Stark now."

A frantic-looking Dianne rushed out and threw herself at Margaret.

"What happened? They say someone got shot."

"I think," Margaret said gently, "I think it was Karen."

"He got Karen, I told you. He's killed her, and he's going to kill me." She was sobbing as a young policeman approached her warily.

"Ma'am, can you tell me anything about this?"

Dianne spun around to face him. "I can tell you the obvious. Some thug shot my sister and killed her."

"She was still alive when the ambulance left. They're rushing her to the hospital," the policeman said.

"Margaret, we've got to find out how she is," Dianne said in a quavery voice, just this side of hysterical.

"Lady, *I've* got to find out who . . ." The policeman was firm.

Margaret said just as firmly, "Mrs. Stark is very upset because her sister has been shot. I don't think she can talk to you right now."

"Now, just a minute, lady . . ."

"I suggest you arrange to have Detective Sam De Vere come around to interview her when he's available. He is a personal friend of hers. And mine. She simply cannot talk now."

"Just give me names," the policeman said.

"The woman who was shot is Karen Reid. She's staying in this building with her sister here, Mrs. Charles Stark."

"You know who did this, Mrs. Stark?"

"I . . . I don't know anything"—Dianne's tears were

flowing, and she was shaking—"except that he thought she was me."

"The shooter thought he was shooting you?" The young policeman was interested. "Who is he?"

"She doesn't know," Margaret said firmly. "The doorman said he ran toward the park, so that's where he is. We've got to find out which hospital . . ."

"New York Hospital is closest," the policeman said kindly. "Or maybe they went to the Bellevue Emergency Room."

"I have to fix my face," Dianne said, "and tell Lourdes where we're going, so she can tell Charlie we won't be dining out tonight." Dianne ran into the building. Margaret followed her but could not stop her. She vanished into the elevator.

"Lady," the doorman said, "I know I got to tell the cops this, but I'm telling you first. The guy who did the shooting, it was the one who hangs around here. The one I told you about."

"The one you might have seen talking to Mrs. Stark's sister?"

"It was her or Mrs. Stark, but that's the one."

"Tell the policeman now." Margaret used her patented "grand lady giving orders" voice, which never failed her. It did not fail her now. The doorman was soon deep in conversation with the young policeman. Dianne was back in only a few minutes, but Margaret didn't want to add to her terror by telling her the doorman's tale.

They found Karen at New York Hospital, but they did not find her alive. Dianne's collapse was complete at hearing the news of her sister's murder. Charlie was located, and was soon there to take Dianne home.

"She kept saying that someone was trying to get her,"

Charlie said, "and I didn't really believe her. Poor Karen, a real nice kid, lots of fun to be around. Dianne is certain that the person who did this had been stalking her and killed Karen by mistake. Well, they did look a bit alike. I'd better get her home fast."

"And maybe hire a bodyguard," Margaret said. "Ah, Charlie. Do you know anything about the man Dianne was married to before you?"

"I knew he existed, but we've never had any contact with him." He faced Margaret. "Do you mean to say that he's behind this?"

"I don't know what I mean to say," Margaret said. "But I'm going to locate De Vere and get his help. Remember that if someone is trying to kill your wife, when it's learned that the wrong person was murdered, that person is maybe going to have another go at killing Dianne."

"I think that would be truly stupid. He should know she'll be protected now, because we can't keep it a secret that it was Karen and not Dianne who was killed. But I'm not without influence," Charlie said. "I'll see if we can make it a random mugging gone wrong while we get the authorities looking into what it really was."

They returned to the Starks' apartment building, which was still cluttered with police, neighbors curious about what had happened, and stray onlookers. Charlie took Dianne upstairs to put her into the care of Lourdes, and Margaret looked around for a cab to take her home.

Suddenly Margaret glimpsed her friend, the homeless man, in police clutches. "You can't do that," she said forcefully to the police surrounding him. "He's done nothing."

"This is police business, lady. He could be dangerous."

"I hope you don't think he was involved in the shooting. This gentleman was with me up the street near Madison when the shooting occurred. We both ran here when we saw people trying to help Miss Reid. I absolutely assure you that he was in no way involved."

"And who would you be?"

"Lady Margaret Priam. I am . . . a friend of Sam De Vere's."

"So you claim to be De Vere's friend?"

"There is no claiming about it. I am, and he will be grateful if you inform him of this incident."

The policeman looked doubtful, but he released his grip on the homeless man. "Don't lose yourself, buddy. We'll need to talk to you."

He shrugged and said, "I hang up at the corner on Madison. You can find me there anytime." To Margaret he said, "Thanks. They coulda roughed me up or locked me up."

"Well, I do know for certain that you had nothing to do with this. Do you know who the man was? The doorman said he was in the area a lot. Have you ever seen him?"

"I've seen a guy hanging around this building for the past couple of weeks. I think maybe he's the one who did the shooting; it kinda looked like him. But we were way down at the corner when it happened, so I didn't get a real good look."

"Neither did I," Margaret said.

"That's a real lousy thing to happen. Lady comes home and some bum tries to rob her but kills her instead."

"It's pretty awful, I agree," Margaret said, "but I think he was out to kill Mrs. Stark, the lady I came back with, and mistook her sister for her."

"I know the lady, Mrs. Stark. I see her on the street sometimes, and sometimes she gives me a handout. She's got a cute baby that she pushes in a carriage, or else it's the Chinese lady."

"That's the one. Look, I have to leave now, but if you see Mrs. Stark out on the street alone anytime, keep a watch over her. I'm afraid he's going to try again."

Chapter 8

Margaret made her way home feeling completely unsettled. She hated to think of poor Dianne cringing in terror through the weekend. And now she didn't even have her sister with her, only the grief of her death. She'd call her later, when Dianne might be calmer, but she'd better think of something to accomplish right now. And the answer was, quite simply, Sam De Vere. She wasn't sure any of the policemen would respond to her demand that they inform him.

She dialed the number of the apartment in Chelsea he shared with Prince Paul—when Prince Paul was in town. So it was only De Vere inhabiting the spacious flat owned by Paul's mother, who asked only a token rent, making it perfect for the always impecunious Paul.

After many rings Margaret was about to give up, and think about calling De Vere at the precinct. She didn't like to bother him at work, and in any event, he was rarely there, so . . .

"Pronto . . ."

"Paul, you're back! It's Margaret."

"I was moments away from calling you," he said. "I only just arrived from Boucan by way of Dallas."

"Surely it wasn't that simple." Boucan was a very small

Caribbean island, politically attached to a larger island with a true international airport, but Margaret somehow imagined there weren't many direct flights to Texas.

"*Cara,* nothing to do with flying is simple anymore. Boucan to Betun, to Miami, to Dallas, to the Newark airport, and then that bus to Manhattan, and a taxi home. My mother failed to provide cab fare from Newark to New York, and she certainly knows how expensive it is." Paul sounded grumpy as he usually did when reflecting on Carolyn Sue's reluctance to hand over large amounts of cash. Paul was simply going to have to learn to live on the modest allowance his mother provided, or make a success of himself in banking, or marry the Honorable Georgina Farfaine and retire to her island, where there were plenty of servants and considerable financial assets.

"But you're back, I'm so glad. We've missed you." Then Margaret added quickly, before they became involved in a conversation about Paul's recent adventures, "Is De Vere in? I have a sort of problem."

"Margaret, you are not going to mention the word 'murder,' are you? You know how that annoys De Vere. And me, for that matter."

"It didn't start out as a murder problem," she said, "but it is one now." She explained about Karen, and Paul was silent for a time.

"I knew her. Remember I took her out once, a year or so ago. Not my type, but very nice. I hate it when things like this happen. De Vere is not in evidence," Paul said. "The place looks as though he hasn't been here for a time. That big plant I bought to beautify the place is quite dead. Have you not spoken with him recently?"

"Actually, I haven't. He was rather closemouthed about his affairs when last we talked. Some case that was taking up his time, but he said nothing about leaving town, or leaving the plant to die."

"After these months in the tropics, I've grown accustomed to having green things growing around me. The tropics condition one to . . . to luxuriant growth."

Margaret thought she detected a faint Caribbean tinge to the slight Italian accent he affected. Could he have gone native in the few months of winter he'd spent lolling beside the pool at Georgina's tanned side?

"It was not a very pleasant plant, after all," Paul said. "I will replace it with something nicer. An hibiscus with red flowers. What is the problem, or is it just the murder?"

"It's more than just a murder," Margaret said, "because I believe the gunman thought he was shooting Dianne. I think someone has been stalking her, and he might try again, but I don't think I can share all the details with you," Margaret said. "Please, please have De Vere ring me if he shows up."

"You have shared much with me, Margaret. It is not the time to change your habits. Perhaps I can help."

Margaret wondered if he could. Paul understood his sex, and he had certainly developed strong romantic attachments to women who might be unavailable, but she did not think he had ever been a stalker of women.

"It's about men who might have an obsession with Dianne Stark," she said.

"*La Bellissima!* Is it her husband? I do not completely trust men who handle large amounts of money for others."

"No, it's not Charlie. But listen, she hasn't been willing to tell me exactly what's wrong, so I'm worried now that Karen has been killed. It appears that someone has been threatening her for some time. It might be her former husband. Did you know that she was married before Charlie?"

Paul did not answer immediately.

"Are you there?" she asked. His silence seemed to indicate that he did know something. But how? Dianne was unlikely to have confided in him, a presentable young man, to be sure, but scarcely material for intimate confidences.

"I am here," he said. "I do know something of this, although I promised Dianne not to speak of it."

Another blow to Margaret's image of herself as Dianne's best friend.

"It was not something Dianne told to me exactly," he said. "I . . . I happened to meet him not too long ago."

"How?" What had Poppy said? A blue-collar type, who worked as a seaman? An unlikely acquaintance for Prince Paul Castrocani.

"An unlikely acquaintance for Prince Paul Castrocani," she said.

"It was quite by accident," he said. "He was hanging about outside the Starks' building when they were having a reception. I was nearly the last to leave, and Dianne came downstairs with me to get a breath of air. She saw a man, and asked me to find out what he wanted. I thought it odd at the time, but when I spoke to him, he said he was an old friend of Mrs. Stark's and was leaving on a long sea voyage, and wanted to say good-bye. She refused to speak to him, and he went away. Then Dianne told me that she had once been married to the fellow. I thought it odd at the time, but she never mentioned the matter again. She asked me not to mention the marriage. I could understand that. For some time my own mother forbade me to mention her marriage to my father, and she seldom mentioned him, except when she wished to make a splash as Principéssa Castrocani."

"How odd," Margaret said. "How long ago?"

"Three or four months ago. Just before I departed for the Caribbean. I remember the weather was bad, and I was eager to leave. Is he the one who is troubling her?"

"Perhaps. When you met him, did he seem threatening?"

Paul chuckled. "Not at all. He was not an imposing figure, and he appeared quite peaceful."

"What did he look like?"

"Not old, not really young. Uncouth to my eyes, sandy hair, no visible scars, although I believe he had a tattoo on his arm. I remember thinking that odd, too. It was a cold evening, but he wore a short-sleeved shirt."

"I think he sent a letter threatening to kill her, and he managed to send her a card marking their wedding anniversary. He seems confused about his feelings for her. And there are others. Do you know Gerald Toth? Antonio Palomino? Well, you probably wouldn't. You've been away, and they're rather recent on the New York scene."

"The name of Gerald Toth is quite widely known," Paul said. "I do not care to admit that I study the stock market or know anything about the computer business, but even in Boucan, newspapers and magazines appear with his name prominently displayed. Georgina is quite devoted to reading *The Financial Times*, even if it arrives weeks out of date. I think this must be an English habit, reading about the home country when one is abroad colonizing another."

Georgina's father, Lord Farfaine, and his family had certainly colonized Boucan, as Margaret knew from personal experience.

"Toth is far richer than even my mother," Paul said. "He is reportedly worth billions. I take notice of that sort of reputation."

"He seems to have established himself in New York for the moment," Margaret said, "and there are rumors that he is interested in Dianne. Don't know how true they are."

"Toth has had an astonishing success in business, and perhaps even Bill Gates has taken notice. If lovely Dianne is seeking entertainment outside of her marriage, he can afford to entertain her well, but I should think he is above making unwelcome advances."

"They would be unwelcome on the face of it. I don't think Dianne is looking beyond Charlie," Margaret said. "Still, someone is making her nervous." She sighed. "It's more likely to be the ex-husband. But rumor has it that Charlie's former wife has returned."

"Well, I know the former Mrs. Stark. She is not a threatening person, although she seemed quite put out that Charlie had left her for Dianne. She complained about his treatment of her for several hours at an otherwise pleasant party I attended. But I think she, too, is above threatening letters, although I have never claimed to understand the workings of the female mind."

"I'm having drinks with Gerald Toth at Elinor Newhall's place tonight, so I'll have a chance to form an opinion. I'm glad to have the information about him, though, since I don't read much about the business world. What about Antonio Palomino?"

"Everyone knows him." Margaret did not miss the contempt in his voice. "He is an international party animal. I believe his principal charm in recent years is an endless supply of cigars from his native land, and perhaps other desirable but illegal substances as well."

"Drugs?"

"I do not know that. You hear all sorts of vicious tales about men who are successful with the opposite sex. In the old days he would wash up on the shores of the Mediterranean when . . ." Paul stopped, and Margaret imagined that he was thinking wistfully of his carefree, all-expenses-paid days when he, too, was an international party animal, and Carolyn Sue was still willing to foot the bills.

"I did not like him," Paul said. "He was not kind to women. Indeed, I remember one occasion at a club in Rome when he took his fists to a pretty little dancer who rejected his attentions. I was young and innocent at the time, so I remember being appalled by his behavior."

Antonio Palomino sounded like a good suspect in the terrorizing of Dianne Stark. "Would he resort to murder? I mean, do men of the world of his type become so obsessed with someone like Dianne that he could wish her dead if he could not have her?"

"These playboys have far too many other delicacies on their plate to worry about one woman, even someone as desirable as Dianne, who have means of retaliation. In the case of the brutalized dancer, my father called in a favor and had him removed from the country. Of course, it helped that the dancer was well connected to a family that had—still has—considerable influence in certain circles. I cannot imagine they were happy about her choice of profession, but nevertheless, family is family. We did not see Antonio again in Rome."

"I wish to meet him," Margaret said.

"No," Paul said, "you do not."

Margaret decided not to argue with him, but to find her own way to Antonio Palomino's side.

"But this matter of Dianne," Paul said. "It sounds dangerous. I think you should not involve yourself directly."

Margaret chose not to argue, and they spoke of Paul's plans. Georgina would join him in New York after a trip home to England, and while marriage was still an option, he was not sure that he could manage it until he had established himself some way in business. "I cannot, after all, live on my mother's fortune forever," he said. Of course he could. Carolyn Sue's fortune was very large. "I feel I am not truly suited to . . . to working. It seems so pointless to arrive at an office every day and then not know what I am doing or why I am doing it. True, Georgina is an heiress with considerable expectations, but in this I am not my father's son. I do not think I could live solely on my wife's money, although it would be nice to know it's there."

"Yet your father managed."

"Even Prince Aldo was not in the end willing to pay the price, which meant attend only to my mother. If I were to fall on my knees and beg her to support me, she would only allow it if I returned to live in Dallas. That is out of the question. If Georgina and I do marry, she would have to live in Dallas as well, and she would hate it. She thrives only in the mists of England or under the tropical sun. Besides, the airport is impossible."

"Surely it is not as impossible as Kennedy or La Guardia," Margaret said. "And remember that Neiman Marcus would be right there on your doorstep, and there are all those pretty Texas girls."

"True," Paul said. "But Neiman's is everywhere now, and I do not easily tolerate big hair."

Chapter 9

After her troubling time with Dianne, and catching up on Paul's adventures, Margaret was exhausted, and could scarcely concentrate on what she would wear to meet Gerald Toth—never mind what she would say to him. And somewhere in the back of her mind she was wondering where De Vere had gone for so long that he hadn't been able to dump some water on Paul's plants.

Indeed, after an almost definite proposal of marriage a few months back, matters between her and De Vere seemed to have settled into a kind of offhand remoteness. And it wasn't all Sam De Vere's doing. She had a lot of reservations about such a commitment, and tried to keep herself otherwise occupied. Still, they had been through a lot together, and she knew her feelings were deep, but were they as deep as marriage required?

"That is the question," she said aloud as she drew a bath. The warm, scented water would wash away her weariness, and she would emerge refreshed and ready for Gerald Toth. As she lay back in the bathtub, she rejected the tailored green silk suit as too high-fashion for an informal gathering, then settled on a rose tunic from Dana Buchman in heavy silk, with paler rose palazzo pants. A bit of gold jewelry. She looked especially good in pink, it suited her pale English complexion and short blond hair. The outfit was just casual enough for cocktails, and even dinner if she could entice him to inviting her out to dine.

As she was touching up her nails after her bath, a sudden feeling of unease washed over her. What a worthless activity all this was. Dressing and primping to meet people with whom she had only the faintest connection. Even without knowing him, she had strong doubts that Gerald Toth could be the one who had shot Dianne's sister and was annoying Dianne. Why, with all the money he supposedly had, he could simply have her kidnapped. But then, he could also arrange to have her killed. All it took was money. However, if Dianne was feeling as low as she appeared to be, an invitation to flee with him on some romantic adventure might easily be an appealing solution. Maybe he believed that a threat could push her into taking flight with him.

Margaret took one last look in the mirror and approved of herself. She hoped that Gerald Toth, the well-known ladies' man, would also approve enough to confide in her about his relationship with Dianne.

She found a taxi to take her the short distance to Elinor Newhall's building on Beekman Place. A number of her friends lived in the area. Elinor's place was a five-story town house, not far from the house where Irving Berlin had lived and died. It had a view of the East River, Margaret remembered, from committee meetings, and all the comforts anyone could desire. The trees along the street had produced delicate, feathery leaves, and the urns guarding the doorways were overflowing with impatiens and petunias. It was still quite light at seven-thirty, but lamps were glowing in all the rooms of the house. The windows were open, and she could hear music and voices from within.

Apparently Elinor had more than a few friends and ac-
quaintances who enjoyed her entertainments while Mr.
Newhall was shuffling the cards on his boys' night out.

A maid answered her ring, and directed her to the second floor, up a very graceful staircase. On the landing she
had no trouble easing into a large room overlooking the
river, and filled with people holding glasses and nibbling
on treats offered by staff passing through with trays of
elaborate canapés. She looked about for Elinor, but saw
only a few people she recognized, ladies from various committees she'd served on, women she'd worked with recently on the designer show house that poor Gloria Anton
had organized last year. Elinor herself was nowhere to
be seen.

"Margaret! Darling!"

Margaret looked around quickly and saw Bobby Henley, an arch-rival of Giovanni's. Bobby was another of
the designers who had been involved in the ill-fated show
house.

"Hullo, Bobby. Is Archer with you?" Margaret said,
hoping that Bobby and Archer were still devoted com-
panions. Things changed so fast nowadays, one could
never be certain one wasn't making some terrible gaffe
by mentioning a relationship that simply everyone knew
had dissolved. "I didn't know you knew Elinor."

"Hello, sweetie. Archer couldn't face another evening
out, but I'm here because every designer in town is making her acquaintance. We're all dying to get our hands on
her place in the Hamptons. I mean, even Godfrey Helms
is dusting off his trashy old chandeliers. But I hear you've
been pushing Giovanni."

"Of course. It's my job," Margaret said. "Have you
seen Elinor about?"

He jerked his head. "She's out on the roof terrace with that nouveau, Gerald Toth. Now, there is a man without an ounce of class, but he's only a close second to that Cuban gangster, Palomino."

"Antonio Palomino is here tonight?"

"He was a short time ago. I don't think he's the sort of person you should consort with. Gerald is another story." Bobby shrugged. "Money makes all the difference, and Gerald is dreamy to look at. Nothing much to say, though. Wit is in short supply."

"I want to meet them both. I've heard so much . . ."

"Our pretty Dianne Stark has been talking, I'll bet. People have been talking. Both of those guys are absolutely wrong for her. I say, did you hear about her troubles? That nice sister of hers got shot."

"I was just up the street when it happened."

Bobby sighed. "What is this city coming to? I'm almost afraid to walk my precious dog these days. Well, come along, I'll introduce you to Gerald, if I can pry him away from Elinor. She's got a real crush on him." Bobby wrinkled his nose. "Unseemly in a woman of her age."

"Since when does age have anything to do with a crush?"

"You know what I mean." Bobby led her through a doorway onto a terrace built atop the ground floor. There were benches and a white railing all around, even several trees forming little shady groves, and pots of highly scented flowers. There was a little fountain playing in the middle of the terrace. Margaret spotted Elinor leaning on the railing with the lights of the Fifty-ninth Street Bridge just twinkling on and a stream of headlights moving to and from Queens on the other side of the river. Standing beside her, with his back to the house, was a tall man with rather longish dark hair. He didn't appear to be anything like the fleeing man who had shot Karen.

Before they approached Elinor, Bobby grabbed Margaret's hand and pushed her into a cloud of cigar smoke, the source of which was a rather paunchy middle-aged man with heavy features. He was wearing a white suit, and looked very much like a slightly dangerous banana republic dictator.

"Margaret, this is Antonio Palomino. Tony, this is Lady Margaret Priam, who has been dying to meet you." Bobby grinned, and looked like a mischievous blond elf.

"It is my great pleasure to make your acquaintance, Doña Margarita." Antonio kissed her hand and bowed, and all Margaret could think of was how right Bobby had been to note that Antonio Palomino was quite unsuitable for Dianne. On the other hand, she could easily imagine him knocking a poor little dancer about. But he was scarcely a romantic-looking Latin, and she could not believe that he had been stalking Dianne. Well, looks could be deceiving, as her old nanny used to remind her when she complained that the blancmange looked "funny."

Bobby managed without much difficulty to steer her away from Antonio Palomino and toward Gerald Toth and Elinor.

"Ah, Margaret," Elinor said. "You made it. Has someone seen to a drink for you? Bobby, fetch whatever Margaret wants. That's a love."

"Elinor's serving a rather decent champagne tonight," Bobby said as he hustled back into the house.

"The lure of a possible decorating assignment has made him an obedient servant," Elinor said, and laughed. "Don't worry about your Giovanni, I haven't made a decision yet, but I'm enjoying the flattering attention from all these designing boys."

Margaret looked up at the tall man, and at the same moment he looked down at her with the most startling blue eyes she had ever encountered. If this was Gerald Toth, the descriptions of him had been inadequate. He was, she thought, quite the handsomest man she had ever seen.

"Gerald, may I present Lady Margaret Priam," Elinor was saying, somewhat unwillingly. "She's been most eager to meet you. Margaret, this is my dear friend, Gerald Toth, of whom you must have heard."

"Well, one does see his name on the financial pages," Margaret said, "although I personally know very little about computers."

"Then, we'll have to correct that," he said, and his voice was as appealing as the rest of him. "I have a little company out in California that is all about computers. What would you like to know?" He took her arm now and guided her a little distance away from Elinor, who, Margaret imagined, wanted to stamp her foot in annoyance.

"I must confess," he said softly, "that I have been hearing your name, and when Elinor said she'd invited you this evening, I changed my plans in order to be here."

"Now, that is flattering," Margaret said. "Whoever could have been mentioning me?"

"Oh, Elinor, and Dianne Stark."

Margaret didn't think it would be this easy to bring the conversation around to Dianne, but here it had been handed to her, just as Bobby was handing her a flute in which champagne bubbles were rising enthusiastically. "Thanks, Bobby."

"Now that you two have already met, I'd better rush to entertain Elinor, who seems a bit put out," Bobby said.

"Oh, I don't think . . ."

"He's right," Gerald Toth said, almost in her ear. "Elinor is quite possessive, and she has attempted to take possession of me, but she doesn't take kindly to interference from other women. Since she's been very good about introducing me around, I allow her some control when it suits me. What do you want to know?"

"I . . . I don't know where to begin," Margaret said, thinking of Karen's body on the sidewalk. "Oh, you mean about computers. Nothing really. I don't have much need for them, and only hope that the people who do need them and on whom I depend know what they're doing. Or the computers do."

"They do, pretty much. To tell the truth, I don't know much about the way they work myself. I do know how to figure out what people think they want, and then get the product and sell it to them. Figuring out has to do with following trends and seeing what's developing, getting the product means hiring a stable of free spirits to build the machines and create the software, and selling it means . . . well, selling it, making people want to shell out the dollars to own it. If the first two steps are handled well, the third is pretty easy. Hello, how are you doing?"

They were interrupted numerous times by men who seemed to want to shake the hand of Gerald Toth, perhaps hoping that his golden touch would rub off on them. And by women of all sorts who made a display of melting under his blue-eyed gaze.

"Oh, dear," Gerald said suddenly, just as Margaret was ready to ask him about his acquaintance with Dianne Stark.

"What is it?"

"I see that Leila Parkins is here. She's a dear girl, but someone I'd rather not have to speak with."

"It's over between you, then?"

Gerald frowned slightly and contemplated Margaret briefly. "Is it such common knowledge that there was something that could be over?"

"Forgive me," Margaret said. "Gossip is the currency of this town, and someone happened to mention something. I've known Leila for years." Margaret peered into the throng of people who were now enjoying the mild spring evening on the terrace. Antonio Palomino was passing out cigars to eager takers, rather like a drug dealer offering very good cocaine for "just a try."

Leila was near the door, surrounded by a crowd. Margaret imagined that her hectic social life was beginning to wear her out. Always a pretty child, she was looking much older than her years.

"It was never anything serious," Gerald said. "I met her in California awhile back on a visit to Los Angeles. I think she was hoping to become a movie star. Starlet. Something. And when I got to New York, out of the blue she looked me up as she was back in town, so we went about a bit. She's much too young for me, but people started linking us somewhat too firmly for my taste. So we agreed to part. That is, I made it clear that we would stop seeing each other. Friendly terms and all that. I'd found someone more to my taste, in any case."

A perfect Dianne opportunity handed to her without hesitation.

"That would be Dianne, of course," Margaret said. She could almost feel Gerald retreating mentally. "I'm sorry, it's none of my business. She's a very dear friend. Did you hear about her tragedy?"

"Tragedy?" He sounded alarmed.

"It happened this afternoon. Some thief shot her sister." Margaret stopped. "That's not quite right. It wasn't a thief. I think it was someone obsessed with Dianne, who wanted to kill her, but killed Karen instead."

"How terrible for her. I must call her. Dianne is a wonderful person," Gerald said. "So genuine, and kind, with real character. You don't find that easily among these society women. And beautiful. I regret she is so happy with her husband, although the few times we shared were very happy times for me."

"Do you see her still?"

"No." Toth seemed sad. "I saw that my attentions to her were disrupting her life. In fact, her husband made that very clear to me. So I regretfully forbade myself to think of her or try to see her. Of course, if she walked onto this terrace now, I'd be at her side immediately. Just for the pleasure of her company for a few moments." Then he added hastily, "If I weren't already with you."

Margaret said carefully, "I suppose you can prove where you were late this afternoon."

Gerald Toth looked at her, then threw back his head and laughed. "Detecting, are you? Elinor said you'd been involved in solving some crimes. My dear Lady Margaret, I was in an office filled with the stodgiest bunch of businessmen I've ever had the pleasure to meet. All of them fine, upstanding citizens. I was definitely not lurking on the streets of one of Manhattan's finest neighborhoods, waiting for a chance to gun down Dianne Stark."

How did he know about where it happened, what had happened?

"I didn't really think it was you, but I had to ask, because people have been talking about you and her . . ."

"Can we leave now? I'll take you someplace for dinner. Have you eaten at Jean-Georges over at Columbus Circle in Donald Trump's newly acquired building? A tremendously wonderful restaurant. Exceptional."

"Jean-Georges never fails in his restaurants," Margaret said, "although I have not been to the new one."

"Done."

"I thought it was impossible to make a reservation."

"Ah," Gerald Toth said. "I have friends in high places."

Chapter 10

Margaret and Gerald were forced to engage in stilted conversation with Leila Parkins before they managed to effect their departure.

"How lovely to see you again, Lady Margaret," Leila cooed. She was well dressed, but the hint of passing years that Margaret had noticed earlier was much more evident at close range. "And you, Gerald." She turned her back on him. "And how is that adorable Prince Paul? I haven't seen him for ages, either."

"He is still adorable," Margaret said. "About to be married." Leila looked a bit crestfallen, as though someone had kindly removed a coveted toy from her hands, but she'd learned the lessons of social interaction well. Married does not mean dead.

"Do you think he'd mind if I called him? There aren't too many of the old gang around anymore."

"I'm sure he'd be delighted to hear from you," Margaret said, although she was not sure about that at all.

Then she felt Gerald Toth's hand on her elbow, a gentle hint to start moving toward dinner.

"I'm sure we'll meet again soon," Margaret said, "if you're back in the city for a time."

Leila wrinkled her pert little nose. "I don't plan to stay

permanently. Mumsy wanted me to come home for a while to help her entertain. She always has that huge party on the Fourth of July, you know, our Independence Day from you people." Leila seemed pleased that Margaret wasn't puzzled by the reference, or offended by being reminded that Americans had dared to declare their independence from the English. "But I do have my career in California to think of."

"Surely she's not serious about a career in films," Margaret said to Gerald as they descended the stairs and walked out into the warm spring night.

"All things are possible in Hollywood, but I believe she sees herself more as a professional celebrity," he said. "Although the bloom is fading." He shrugged. "I didn't bring my car. I hope you don't mind a taxi."

"Taxis are a blessing, whereas cars in Manhattan are not," Margaret said.

He quickly flagged down a cab, and they rocketed away across town through Central Park to the West Side. Margaret was very conscious of his closeness in the lumpy backseat, and when she glanced at his beautiful profile, she felt an unexpected weakness come over her. It surprised her, and she wondered if she was developing her own little crush on Gerald Toth.

As they crossed Fifth Avenue, Margaret said, "Dianne lives a few blocks north of here."

"I know," Gerald said. He looked at her from the corner of his eye. "What I don't know is why you keep trying to turn the conversation to Dianne. I do find her charming and attractive, and I consider her a friend, but I don't have a deep relationship with her. Gossip notwithstanding."

"I'm sorry," Margaret said. "She's been on my mind

because of what happened today. And she's been upset about this stalker thing, but she won't really confide in me. I guess I'm just looking for reasons."

"I did have one rather odd conversation with her a couple of months ago. She wanted to know whether I had security arrangements, and what they were," Gerald said. "Well, I don't, except that I sometimes hire a bodyguard when I travel abroad to places where kidnapping millionaires is a national hobby. I don't think that was what she meant.

"I asked her what the problem was, but she hedged. I supposed at the time that she was worried about the safety of the little boy. People do heist kids of wealthy parents for ransom, although usually it never works out for either the heister or the heisted."

Margaret said carefully, "She believes someone is planning to kill her, and after what happened to her sister, it looks as though she was right."

Gerald actually laughed and lifted Margaret's hand to his lips. She felt a little thrill when he kissed her hand. "I think you society women read too many mysteries and watch too much television. People don't set out to kill perfectly nice young matrons who don't have an enemy in the world. I'm sure the sister must just have been in the wrong place at the wrong time. Dianne's not into drugs, is she? I never detected anything like that in my brief association with her."

"Of course not." Margaret decided not to mention the ex-husband. "Although she did say she'd been taking medication for her nerves."

Gerald grinned, very appealingly, and his smile seemed to light up the dim taxi. He dropped her hand.

"You see? Perhaps it's some kind of paranoid reaction to the medication."

Yes, Margaret thought, but I saw the letter. I saw Karen's body being taken away. What she said was, "I'm quite convinced that there have been threats."

"I honestly know nothing of this. I'm sorry that for some reason you think that I am involved." He took her chin in his hand and gently forced her to look at him. "I hope you haven't really been thinking that I have been threatening Dianne. The spurned lover? The rich man who won't take no for an answer?" Margaret shook her head, and he released her chin. "I should think that scum Palomino would be a more likely suspect. An ugly little man who thinks he's both attractive and powerful. Do you know about him?"

"I do. I had been forbidden to try to meet him, but I managed to do so tonight. Briefly. I did not find him appealing, and he did not mention Dianne. I think she would not find him of interest, and I suspect he would understand that Dianne was . . . was in a different class. Unreachable."

"I saw him at Elinor's place tonight. So you decided that I was a more likely suspect. Someone more in Dianne's class. Have I convinced you of my innocence?" That smile again, and the feel of his body close to hers.

"Yes. I won't mention it again."

"Good, because here we are. I don't want to spoil what promises to be a superb dinner with talk of threats."

The taxi lurched to a stop at the doors of what had once been the Gulf & Western Building on Columbus Circle, and was now a grandiose condo/hotel project belonging to Donald Trump. The restaurant was a brightly lit wedge of windows on the ground floor facing Columbus Circle and a decorative array of fountains and a huge metal globe.

"I hope you're hungry," Gerald said. "We'll do the tastings menu, and see what wonders Jean-Georges has contrived in his kitchen."

Gerald seemed to be known, and they were immediately seated. The other diners had the aura of money, and a few even nodded to Gerald, no doubt stockbrokers who had profited from his success, or contented computer users who were grateful that he had contrived to sell them the machine of their dreams.

Margaret admired the white china with different geometric shapes in various colors. She sipped the crisp Chardonnay Gerald ordered. She savored the steady parade of little dishes they were served: fried zucchini blossoms, scallops with caramelized cauliflower, a porcini mushroom tart, squab with foie gras on a corn cake, bits of lobster, garlic soup with frogs' legs, and much more. It was better than anything she'd ever eaten, and by the time the little scoops of ice cream arrived, she could barely eat another bite.

All the while Gerald spoke entertainingly of his early years in business, getting his company started, how he avoided being gobbled up by Bill Gates, how he created his breakthrough product. He talked of the pleasures of life in Northern California, even about a marriage that had failed because he was too busy creating an empire to attend to his wife. "I've learned my lesson there," he said. "I intend to marry again. When I find the right one. And you?"

"Me? Ah, I don't know that I'll marry again. My first was over years and years ago." She saw him looking at her intently, and felt a tiny prick of guilt when she thought of De Vere.

"I meant, rather, what about you? How did you end up in New York City? I see you riding to hounds and shooting pheasants somewhere in rainy old England."

So she described Priam's Priory, growing up in the haunted old Tudor house that had once been home to a crowd of monks before the dissolution of the monasteries by Henry the Eighth. She told about strict nannies and governesses, of being sent to Switzerland to finish her schooling, of debutante years and marriage, and finally of making her way to America, to be taken up by the society folks who just couldn't restrain their glee at having a genuine title in their midst.

"My father, the Earl of Brayfield, died some years ago, and my mother, the countess, shortly thereafter. The title is in the hands of my feckless brother, who seems intent on marrying a barmaid to continue the line. The estate still exists, although I see my brother turning it into a retreat for businessmen or a haven for tourists to keep it in the family. You know, a tarted-up bed-and-breakfast, with breakfast featuring an earl, or just a quid for a tour of the house, and a view of the library where the ghost shows up unpredictably, a look around the grounds, which aren't all that unusual, but so pleasant. I really am more of a country girl than a city girl, as long as it's the English countryside. I couldn't figure out a way to make a living there, and believe me when I say that the upper classes have as much need to earn money as the lower, so here I stay. Not that I have much of a living here, but at least I get the occasional free meal. I might end up going home."

"Don't run away yet," Gerald Toth said, and looked at

her so intently with those extraordinary blue eyes that she almost dropped the chocolate-laced cookie she was about to sample.

"I . . . I hadn't planned on going anywhere," she said.

"Excellent. I suggest we dine again on Monday. At Jean-Georges's other place, Vong. I'll have someone check to be sure it's open on Mondays, but even if it isn't, I'll pick you up at eight, if you tell me where you live." Although she neither accepted nor offered regrets, it seemed that the matter was settled. "Now, I do wish I had my car," he said. "We could drive about a bit. I love looking at New York at night, the lights in the skyscrapers and the flow of traffic along the avenues."

"I really should be getting home. I want to check in with Dianne to see that she has calmed down." This was not strictly true. What she really wanted was to get away from the overpowering attraction of Gerald Toth. She wanted space and time to try to think about Sam De Vere, rather than this stranger who seemed to be having an unexpected effect on her. She easily imagined now that Dianne too had readily felt his appeal, and Elinor Newhall as well.

"I wish I were free to see you this weekend," he said, "but I have some business matters to attend to, and . . ." He stopped, and added sheepishly, "I guess that sort of thing is what broke up my marriage."

"As it happens, I have a number of engagements myself this weekend, but I look forward to Monday."

And the truth was, she truly did.

Chapter 11

The next day, Thursday, the day of the committee meeting, Margaret reached Elinor Newhall's building on Beekman Place a few minutes before two. Gerald had dropped her off the night before at her apartment building, when, of course, he had, in the most gentlemanly fashion, kissed her gently on the cheek as he handed her in to the doorman, but she hadn't stopped thinking of him. The idea that they would meet again on Monday gave her a definite thrill. It had been too late to call Dianne after Gerald left, but she had tried to reach Dianne this morning, only to be told by the answering machine that no one was able to take her call. She trusted Charlie to see that Dianne was comforted and sedated while the solemn arrangements for Karen's funeral were carried out by his devoted underlings.

Several of the committee ladies had already arrived, and Margaret noted with considerable distress the piles of envelopes to be addressed laid out on tables. It seemed to her that she had over the past few years spent rather too many hours writing out names and addresses of people she knew quite well, and stuffing the envelopes with engraved pleas to write a check, come to a dinner or dance, take a tax deduction to the extent allowed by law. If this was what made poor Dianne feel worthless, she had been right. Margaret thought that it must be her well-formed italic handwriting that got her put on the invitations sub-committee every time she offered to help a charity project.

Terry Thompson waved merrily, and Margaret went to sit beside her. Margaret was pleased to see that Terry had decided to change the mistaken red hair she had fancied for far too long, and was now a mellow honey blonde. It was a distinct improvement. Elinor's uniformed maid asked what she could bring for Margaret.

"Iced tea," Margaret said, although she had never been able to understand the appeal of weak tea loaded with great lumps of ice. But it was too warm this afternoon for hot tea, and she feared that anything alcoholic—such as Dianne's beloved Campari—would put her into a doze and cause her *C/T* and *S/T* ligatures to blot. A carbonated drink would probably cause unladylike belches.

"How *are* you?" Terry asked. "You look *divine*! And isn't it just *terrible* about Dianne's poor sister?" Terry had taken to speaking in italics, a most unnerving development. "Did you hear that I'll be chairing the committee for a *wonderful* new charity? It has something to do with planting *trees* in grubby old neighborhoods, so the *poor* will have a bit of *lovely* shade next summer or however long it takes for the trees to grow."

Margaret hadn't heard, but she knew what was coming next.

"And certainly I'll want *you* to serve with me. You're such a *good* worker."

Margaret did not wish to commit herself, but she knew that Terry was not easily turned aside.

"I have some other commitments coming up, and I

may have family business in England," Margaret said untruthfully, "so I'll need the particulars before I say yes."

"I had planned to ask *darling* Dianne Stark," Terry said, "but she won't feel like doing *anything* social for a time, will she? I suppose she won't be here today."

"I definitely think not," Margaret said.

"She hasn't been coming to many meetings of this committee, has she? I mean, even when she doesn't have a personal *tragedy* to deal with."

"She has a good deal of business to attend to, and she is so attentive to her little boy," Margaret said. "Now she'll be dealing with her sister's death."

"I suppose you could call it business," Terry said, "but I call it running around behind her husband's back."

"That's not true," Margaret said. The least she could do for Dianne was defend her reputation in her absence. "I don't know how these rumors get started."

"Margaret dear, everyone knows. Why, Elinor herself mentioned it." Terry was a good-hearted woman, and seemed distressed to learn that the rumors were untrue. "I promise you, I haven't been spreading rumors, it's just what other people have said."

"Then, they're saying something that is not the truth." Margaret picked up a sheet of names and addresses, and got out her fountain pen. "God, I hate addressing these things."

"I could make you dinner chairlady," Terry said in an effort to atone for repeating gossip about Margaret's best friend. "You'd get to interview the caterers and decide what *fabulous* food we'll get to eat." Margaret had a momentary recollection of Jean-Georges's porcini mushroom tart. She didn't think the great Jean-Georges Vongerichten catered gala dinners for trees. "Or *flowers*!" Terry went on. "You'd be *wonderful* at that, and we *must* have good flowers, if we're raising money for trees. You know, *growing* things. We might even decorate the place with lovely little *bonsai*. Tiny trees on every table!" Terry sounded quite elated by the prospect. Margaret concentrated on writing out the address of a very old, but very connected lady who hadn't been well enough to attend so much as the opening of an envelope for several years. She always sent a check, however.

Several other committee ladies drifted in and settled themselves to gossip—mostly about the murder of Dianne's sister—and sip drinks carried in by the maid. Now and then she caught Gerald's name being bandied about, and there were covert looks at Margaret, who continued to write serenely. A number of the ladies had attended Elinor's cocktail party the night before, and were extremely well trained in creating fantasies that linked money and a title. Then the chairlady herself appeared in a very nice Prada outfit, Margaret noted.

"Ladies, ladies. We have a lot to do today," Elinor said briskly. "Business first, and then there will be time to chat. I need reports from all the sub-chairs so we'll know where we're at." They came to order.

Margaret listened with complete boredom to reports about the venue, the food, the orchestra, the publicity, the distinguished names enlisted as patrons to impress potential attendees. There were quite a few titles, spurious and genuine, among the patrons and benefactors of the charity, and that would go a long way toward making the festivities desirable to the untitled and the social climbers, who delighted in getting on a first-name basis with a countess or even a baroness. The men liked the former high elected officials, and the ambassadors who had lost their postings when a new party seized the White House. The committee ladies lightly applauded the names from filmdom and the stage who had promised to attend. Celebrities were very high on helping to feed the foodless, no doubt because they were half ashamed of the plenty they enjoyed. Margaret could almost taste Jean-Georges's garlic soup that Gerald had praised highly.

At a pause in the proceedings, Elinor came over to Margaret and whispered, "You and Gerald slipped away so quietly last evening that I didn't even know you were gone until Leila Parkins told me." Her tone was not friendly. "Although he mentioned more than once that he was eager to meet you."

"How has he heard about me?"

"I told you that Dianne had mentioned you as her dearest friend, and of course, you know everybody worth knowing, so your name has probably come up often enough."

My name, Margaret thought. As if a courtesy title gave one substance and worth. And what a worthless thing it was to be Lady Margaret. In England, where people had actually known her father and knew of Priam's Priory and its long history, it was a bit more important to be Lady Margaret Priam, because it attached her to a particular class and place in a country where one's class still influenced how one was viewed. It did give one a kind of worth back home, and maybe it was time to think of moving back there. But De Vere would never settle in England. He loved the streets of New York, and probably would go no further afield than a homestead on Long Island or in New Jersey. On the other hand, it was pleasant to hear from a third party at least that Dianne claimed her as her closest friend.

After listening to the droning reports and writing out addresses for half an hour, Margaret had had enough and put down her pen. "Elinor, I have another appointment that I couldn't reschedule. Very important. I've finished all the *A*'s, and I'm halfway through the *B*'s."

Elinor looked displeased. Margaret wasn't her favorite today, for a number of reasons.

"I could take some of the lists and envelopes home and finish tonight," Margaret said, seeing her commission from Giovanni vanishing if Elinor, in her displeasure, decided to choose a decorator other than Giovanni for the summer place, especially since Bobby had indicated that simply everyone was lining up for a shot at the Hamptons house. "I'm so sorry."

"I understand," Elinor said grudgingly. "You must have been shaken by the shooting. Somebody told me you were actually there when it happened. Well, we have quite a few others to take up the slack today, even though Dianne couldn't make it. But perhaps if you did take a few boxes of envelopes away and returned them to me on Monday, we'll be able to keep to our schedule."

Margaret prepared to flee, loaded down with a hundred envelopes and a handful of lists. But as she made her farewells, the maid plucked at her sleeve.

"Excuse me, Lady Margaret, there is a telephone call for you," the maid said. "She says she is a friend, a Mrs. Stark. It sounded urgent."

The maid led her to an alcove with a telephone, and Margaret took the call. Dianne's voice was trembly, and she sounded as though she were on the brink of hysterics.

"What's the matter?" Margaret asked.

"Lourdes," Dianne said, catching her breath. "Someone attacked her. She was coming back from the park with Chip. I don't know what to do, after . . . after what happened to Karen."

"Is she hurt? Is Chip all right? Wasn't someone supposed to be with her?"

"Edgardo was a little way behind them. A man jumped her and knocked her to the ground. Then Edgardo went after him, and he got up and ran into the park and got lost himself. There's a policeman here at the building, but I'm not allowed out."

"Then, you've talked to the police."

"No," she said slowly. "I haven't felt up to it, but Charlie said someone was on duty in case the fellow who killed Karen came back and the doorman recognized him."

"How did Lourdes get past the policeman?"

"I guess no one thought she was in danger, so no one paid any attention to her leaving with the baby in the stroller. Edgardo didn't get a look at the man. Chip wasn't hurt, Lourdes is just plain mad. No damage was done, but this is what I've been afraid of."

"I was just leaving here. I'll be there with you in a few minutes. And Dianne, this time we have to talk to the authorities and tell them everything that's been going on. You can't wait for friendly old De Vere to come around and chat. I know Charlie would agree. You can't spend your life held hostage by a crazy man. And you have to think of Chip's safety above all."

"I know," Dianne said. She sounded calmer. "I guess I know what I have to do."

Margaret wondered exactly what it was that Dianne meant. Talk to the police, certainly. Persuade Charlie to hire protection. She walked down to Forty-ninth Street and found a cab to take her to the Starks' building. Margaret knew what she had to do, and that was to reach De Vere without delay.

The doorman allowed her to go upstairs without stopping, saying only that Mrs. Stark had notified him that she was coming. Margaret wished that Edgardo or the doorman could identify Lourdes' assailant as similar in appearance to the man who had left the card for Dianne, and maybe hook him up somehow to the man who had murdered Karen. She thought perhaps the questions might better come from a cop like De Vere, or even from Dianne herself, who as a tenant (and probably someone who gave handsome cash gifts to the help at Christmas) would be more persuasive than Margaret.

Dianne herself answered the door. She had been crying, and looked uncharacteristically a mess, even though she apparently had had a chance to visit a hairdresser and get rid of the reddish rinse. Or maybe she'd done it herself. "Thank goodness, you're here," she said. "Lourdes has taken to her room, and I'm minding Chip in the living room." She strode away, and Margaret followed.

Chip was caged in what looked like a high-tech playpen, gurgling unconcernedly as he poked at a colorful animal mobile that hung from a supple stick attached to the side of the playpen. Idiotic children's songs were playing on a CD in the background.

"Here's Auntie Margaret to see Chipper," Dianne said, and Margaret winced. She had no desire to be any child's "auntie." She was not, for her sins, a baby person. Once, long ago, she had had a child, but the happiness of that time, when she still had a husband at her side, evaporated quickly when it became clear that the baby was damaged beyond repair, and would not see her childhood, let alone adulthood. Since then Margaret had avoided relationships with children, and had no wish to reproduce again. Yet Chip was undeniably an adorable infant, just beginning to talk and even make some sense. He had sturdy legs and a crown of golden hair that curled the way his mother's did. The song began again, and Chip kicked his feet in time to the music.

"Hullo, Chipper old sport," Margaret said. Chip seemed to recognize his name and gurgled some more.

"He just loves music," Dianne said. "I think that's a good thing. As soon as he's old enough, I'm going to let him try all sorts of instruments, to see if there's anything he particularly takes to. It would be nice to have a musician in the family. Charles and Zoe's older boy plays the guitar very well, and Charlie was in a marching band in college, so maybe there's a Stark musical gene that's found its way to Chip."

"Dianne, we've got to talk about the murder and the attack on Lourdes."

Dianne's smile was gone, and her shoulders slumped. "I guess we have to. But I was thinking, maybe it was just some mugger who decided to have a go at Karen and then Lourdes. Nothing to do with me or Chip." The thought seemed to cheer her.

"I think," Margaret said, "putting it together with the other things that have happened, we shouldn't dismiss it that easily. Listen, Dianne. You've got to tell me. Can this have anything to do with your ex-husband?"

Dianne hesitated. "You know about him? How? I never told you about him."

"People talk. You should know that."

"I simply can't believe that he would hurt a child or a defenseless woman like Lourdes. Or shoot Karen. He knew her and liked her. Maybe even too well."

"And he once liked you." Margaret frowned at the implications of Dianne's comment about Karen and the ex-husband.

"I have to admit that when I got that letter and the calls started, and the gifts, and that card on our anniversary, I was sure he was coming after me again."

"Again?"

"A couple of years ago, he got in touch with me. He'd seen my name in Poppy's column. I certainly never dreamed that he'd be reading a society gossip column. I had no idea that he was in New York. Our life together was over almost before it began. He was a merchant seaman, and he was always away on some ship. That's when I went into the airlines, so I wouldn't have to sit home alone for months on end and wait for him. We separated by mutual agreement. It was polite and civilized. I guess they don't love you when they want to break it off, and then do when it's finally over. Or maybe they love you and hate you at the same time. Anyhow, I had a busy career, and then I met Charlie on a flight back from Paris, and I knew right away Charlie was the one for me."

"And what happened when you two met again?"

"Nothing happened, not when I saw him the first time. He needed money, and I guess he thought he could blackmail me or something. But there was nothing I could be blackmailed for. Charlie knew about my first marriage, and we agreed never to talk about it. So I sent him on his way, although he wasn't pleased about it. Now I'm afraid he's back, and this time he's not going away easily."

"But you saw him again, quite recently."

"How do you know that I saw him just a short time ago?"

"Paul told me about the time he was outside this building after some party." Dianne looked momentarily relieved. "Dianne, he's been here for months, so we can be sure it's him, and not Gerald Toth or Antonio who's been bothering you. And I think you've seen him in the past few days."

Dianne looked disdainful. "I had to do something to stop him. I didn't succeed. And men like those other two don't have to harass a woman. Women are eager to fall on top of Gerald's pile of money without even being asked. Tony can charm . . . a . . . a pigeon down from a statue, even if he's not the most attractive man you'll ever meet. And besides, I'm not exactly the ultimate love goddess who causes men to lose their minds."

"Whatever," Margaret said. "The first thing to do is to get De Vere's advice. I know there are all kinds of laws now about stalkers, and there certainly are laws about killing someone in cold blood. Even if he didn't murder Karen, you could probably get the courts to forbid him to come near you, or your family. And if the police find him, he'll be arrested for Karen's murder."

"It would be so upsetting for Charlie," Dianne said.

"Dianne," Margaret said sternly, "being upset about a murder is perfectly reasonable."

Then Dianne sighed. "Go ahead. Speak to De Vere. I know we're going to have a lot of other police questioning us, but Sam will know how to handle it diplomatically. I just can't stand any more of this."

Chip decided that not enough attention was being paid to him, and he started to whine. Dianne scooped him up and cuddled him.

"I'm going home to try to locate De Vere," Margaret said. "Just be careful until we get it straightened out. It's going to be okay, trust me."

Chapter 12

Sam De Vere, when Margaret finally reached him, listened seriously to her tale of Dianne's harassment, and more seriously to the tale of Karen's murder.

"It's not much to go on," he said, "and we don't know for certain that the person who's been bothering Dianne is also the murderer and possibly her ex-husband, but that letter is worrying. If no one can identify the man who knocked the nanny down, or the person who brought the card, or who sent the flowers or is making the phone calls, it's going to be hard to get something done. It could be different people."

"You don't believe that, do you?"

"Not really. I'm going to have a look at what the guys have turned up. If there are questions to be asked of Dianne, I'll try to arrange to be the one who does the asking."

"That's all I'd hoped for," Margaret said.

"Maybe Charlie's former wife is peeved about something and is trying to upset the marriage," De Vere said. "Didn't you tell me that Charlie left her, and then she ran off with a younger man? Since the bloom is off that romance, she could be pining for her old place on Fifth Avenue."

"Oh, I don't think Charlie would take her back, and I

don't think Zoe would dress up like a man to shoot Dianne. That's what happened, don't you think? He thought it was Dianne. People say they looked alike. Zoe has been living in Seattle, and only came back to New York recently. Several people have mentioned that she's back in the city."

"There, you see? She could be a possible suspect."

"I think Dianne's been troubled for some time. Zoe's only recently back, and she couldn't have been doing it by long distance. Besides, I still don't see New York society ladies slaughtering people on the street."

De Vere was silent for a moment. "I can't believe that you of all people said that."

"Well," Margaret said defensively, "poison and accidental falls are rather different."

"Not to my mind," De Vere said. "Maybe it is these other fellows who you say are enamored of Dianne. That's not preposterous, she's a great-looking woman, although how they think unwanted approaches will help their romantic case, I don't know."

"You wouldn't behave that way with me, would you?"

She could hear the smile in his voice. "I don't have to. I've got you all sewn up." Margaret felt a sudden pang of guilt as the image of Gerald Toth flashed through her mind. Those blue eyes of his haunted her.

Her voice was shaky when she spoke. "But what should Dianne do?"

"You sound strange. Are you okay? Nobody's bothering you, are they?"

"No, no. Of course not. Who'd bother me?"

"Tell Dianne to keep an exact record of everything that happens. Time and date of phone calls, deliveries, anything she finds suspicious. The police need records to show a pattern of harassment, frequency, nature of the acts, that sort of thing. And it may help catch the killer as well. She shouldn't go out alone . . ."

"She already doesn't, and she doesn't allow the nanny to take the little boy out without someone with her. Only this time it didn't work as planned."

"Keep me posted. I suppose Charlie could afford a bodyguard, if it comes to that."

"When do I get to see you? It's been days."

"Sweetheart, I go to Albany in the morning on business, gone all weekend. Paul and I are having a guys' night out before I leave, so he can tell me about the islands and that woman he's attached himself to, and what his mother is up to. How about Monday?"

"Can't," Margaret said, suddenly deeply regretting the upcoming dinner date with Gerald Toth. "Later in the week?"

"Sure," he said. "I'll call you from Albany. I've missed you."

"I've missed you, too. Sam, wait. Can't you please change your plans and not go to Albany? Or at least cancel Paul tonight. He'd understand. I'm afraid, and Dianne is terrified. There's a murderer out there. Aren't the police supposed to catch criminals and comfort the public? Like me?"

"I'm sure there are any number of my colleagues searching for the murderer," De Vere said. "I can't do it all. But I should be able to comfort my public. Let me see what I can do about canceling Albany. I might even be able to cancel Paul, in which case, I'll call you."

Margaret sat quietly in her darkening living room, thinking about De Vere. So he thinks he's got me all sewn up. He's right, except . . . How would it all work out with

Gerald? And will I finally marry De Vere? I can't imagine it at the moment. I'd worry more than I do now that he'd be killed or injured. And however empty this life of mine is, I don't want to leave New York. I don't want a home in the suburbs and a dog and a vegetable garden. I will not become Martha Stewart and make cunning little things out of grosgrain ribbon. I won't get the post-holer out of the garage and build a trellis and prune the cherry trees.

She told herself to calm down. Perhaps Paul would have some free time this weekend to escort her somewhere fun. She'd call him in the morning, and might even find out then if De Vere had gone away after all.

She went to bed thinking more of De Vere and less of Gerald Toth. Somehow this was a comfort to her.

Before she had a chance to call Paul on Saturday morning, however, she received a rather unexpected call.

"Charles Stark here, Margaret. May I speak with Dianne?"

Margaret hesitated. "Dianne isn't here."

"She must be . . . She said . . . Margaret, don't try to cover for her. Just put her on the phone."

"Charles, really. She's not here. I saw her yesterday afternoon at your place, and that's the last time we talked. She didn't say anything about going someplace."

"Well, she's gone. Where? Who would she go to if not to you?"

"Did you have a . . . a fight?" Margaret was cautious about getting involved in a domestic argument.

"No, no, of course not. I came home as soon as she called about Lourdes. Did you hear about that? When I got here, Lourdes said Dianne had retired to her room, so I left her alone. She was still terribly upset about Karen.

Then I fell asleep watching TV, so it wasn't until this morning that I went to look for her. She wasn't in her room, and I assumed she'd gone out early. Now I'm beginning to worry, so I thought of you."

"Did anything happen yesterday besides the Lourdes incident to upset her?"

"Nothing that I know of. Oh, Lourdes showed me a huge bunch of roses she'd received, but there was no card. Lourdes said one of the men from the building had brought them up. The housekeeper received them and put them in water. I don't know if Dianne told you, but we've been getting unexpected deliveries, phone calls at odd times. It's made Dianne jumpy. Maybe the roses upset her."

"Did she take anything with her? Clothes, makeup, the things she'd take if she were going away on a trip? Her passport?"

"I don't know. I could ask the housekeeper, but she won't be in until tomorrow. I asked her to come in even though it's Sunday because Dianne has been so upset. Lourdes might know if things are missing."

"I'm sure she just went off for some quiet time, Charles. She'll probably be back today. Or she'll call you, she might be trying to call you now. If you'd like, I'll ask around and see if anyone knows where she is."

"Probably better you than me," Charles said. "You wouldn't have to say that she's missing from home, just that you need to talk to her."

"Charles, have you called the police?"

"Police? What for?"

Because your wife is missing, you silly man. Margaret thought it, but did not speak the words aloud. "I mean, keep that option open, in case she doesn't turn up. They'll be able to keep watch for her."

"Do you think she's really run away? She hasn't been herself lately."

"I don't think anything, except that she might have wanted to be alone for a day or so." Margaret tried to sound as untroubled and matter-of-fact as possible, but she was deeply worried. What if the person who was harassing her had something to do with this? What if Dianne felt she had to run for her life? Too many what-ifs, and maybe by now Sam was hundreds of miles away in Albany. She had no one to ask for advice.

"Charlie, are you still there?"

"I am, and I have to tell you that I am worried sick."

"I'll see if anyone knows where she is, and call you as soon as I know anything."

"Thank you, Margaret. Maybe your friend De Vere could help."

"He's out of town," Margaret said. "But he promised to help deal with the murder. I'll call you." She rang Poppy immediately.

"Poppy, I know it's early, but I need your help." Poppy Dill sounded mostly still asleep when she answered, and not too happy about being awakened.

"It's never too early to hear from you," Poppy said graciously. "What can I do?"

Silently thanking the Spirit of Gossip for granting Poppy the ability to remain silent when necessary, Margaret said, "I was wondering if you had any idea where Dianne might be."

"Dianne? Why would I know that? What's wrong?"

"Nothing much. I was trying to locate her. I saw her last evening, but now she's gone off somewhere. She's been pretty shaken by everything, but she didn't say anything about going away."

"Do you mean she's run away? Disappeared?"

"I hardly think it's come to that." Margaret tried to sound unconcerned, but Dianne had said that she knew what she had to do. "Please don't spread it around to anyone. Do you think she might have gone off with one of her admirers? Gerald or Antonio?" She didn't think that Dianne had turned to Antonio Palomino, or even that Gerald would have accepted the responsibility for her.

Poppy said, "I could ask if they are in the city."

"Gerald is here. I dined with him the other evening, but he said he had business to attend to this weekend."

"Gerald and you? What am I hearing?"

"Oh, Poppy. I met him at Elinor Newhall's place, and he persuaded me to join him at Jean-Georges."

"Divine restaurant, or so everybody says."

"It is, and there's nothing more to be said about Gerald and me. Anyway, Dianne is the one we should be concerned about. Is there anyone she might have gone to, where she could hide out for a couple of days?"

"You're about the best friend she has, Margaret. If she didn't come to you, maybe she just found herself a nice hotel."

"Of course." Margaret felt greatly relieved. The Villa d'Este. A Campari and soda from room service, a nice soft bed, and solitude. A place where no stalker or murderer would think of looking for her. "If you hear anything, please let me know, Poppy. And I'll keep you posted. Dianne has been greatly troubled lately, but I think I know where she must be."

But she wasn't at the Villa d'Este, at least not as Mrs. Charles Stark. Margaret called a few more nice hotels, but had no success with them, either. Then Poppy rang her back around noon to say that both Antonio Palomino and Gerald Toth were safely in their places of residence, and there was nothing to indicate that either was trysting with Dianne.

"I don't understand," Margaret said. "How does one just disappear?"

"I don't understand," Charles said when she called him to say she hadn't located Dianne. "How does a person just disappear? I'm beginning to worry. She left her credit cards and her passport behind, but she probably has plenty of cash. She tends to keep a goodly amount on hand. Lourdes says she thinks a couple of outfits are missing, but she can't be sure. The doorman didn't see her leave this morning, and I'm waiting for the afternoon man, who might have seen her leave yesterday evening. I . . . I've called the hospitals, but there's no one like Dianne who's unidentified. And I called the police, who weren't very helpful. They are not greatly concerned about adult women who haven't been seen for less than a day. Can't you locate De Vere and ask him what to do?"

"I'll try," Margaret said. "Could you find out where those roses came from? I'd suggest La Vie en Rose on Madison. Maybe she was upset about who the sender was. The florist might know something."

Charles seemed grateful to have something to do.

Finally she had a moment to call Paul. She explained the latest Dianne crisis, and Paul said the word she hadn't dared think about.

"Kidnapped, do you think? The ex-husband spirits her away, thinking Charles would pay a ransom."

"He would, of course, if he thought it would get her

back unharmed. But I don't like to suggest the possibility of kidnapping to him. He's upset enough as it is."

"If she's been kidnapped, someone will eventually get in touch with Charles."

"And we'll be able to find out something from the doorman, who might have seen her yesterday. Even if he didn't, there could be others who saw her—a cabdriver who picked her up. She's surely not simply walking the streets in her own neighborhood."

"Maybe she is," Paul said. "Or maybe she took a bus down Fifth to the Village. Or walked uptown to the Metropolitan Museum, and is even now gazing at some fine Renaissance portraits. Maybe she's trying on outfits at Bendel's or Bergdorf's. I will bet that she's home before nightfall."

"Can you take me some place where I could meet Antonio Palomino?"

"Absolutely not. He is not anyone you need to know."

"I know him already. I met him the other day. Not my type." She decided not to mention meeting Gerald Toth. "I feel that I have to do something," Margaret said. "I want to find Dianne."

"I, too, would feel better if she were located," Paul said. "I will sit quietly now and try to think of places she might be."

"Paul, if De Vere should ring up, please tell him he must call me. He said he was going to Albany."

"That is true, he planned to, but he did not go in the end," Paul said. "He is out now on some business. I think it may have to do with Dianne's sister. But he will return." Nothing that Gerald Toth could buy her could ever give her such pleasure as hearing that De Vere was still in Manhattan.

"I need him as soon as possible. Let me know if you get any ideas. I think I'll walk about, and if she's to come to rest anywhere but at home, I'm sure it will be the d'Este."

"Let us meet there in the lobby bar. It is nearly noon," Paul said. "I can be there in half an hour. We will put our heads together, and because they all know that I am Carolyn Sue's son, the bartender will give us free drinks, and the waiter will bring us bowls and bowls of cashews. The dining room will feed us, and we will keep watch for Dianne."

Chapter 13

Margaret tried again at the front desk of the Villa d'Este to determine whether Dianne had chosen to hide out there.

The desk clerk was very nice, very polite, but refused to provide any information. Margaret caught sight of Paul surveying the lounge as she strolled to the house phones. The operator might connect her immediately if Dianne was somewhere in one of the luxurious suites. (Carolyn Sue made certain that all the suites were the height of luxury.) But it turned out that Dianne Stark was not a guest at the hotel. Was Lady Margaret sure that she had the correct name?

Margaret mentally snapped her fingers. Of course Dianne wouldn't register under her own name. She tried to think what name she would choose, but that would mean she would have to have the proper identification to check in.

"Right on time," she said as she approached Paul's back. He was staring at a glass of red wine the waiter had just served him, and was carefully picking out the cashews from a bowl of mixed nuts. Not a healthy lunch for a growing prince. She slid into the chair beside him. "Do you think that Dianne would be using her maiden name?"

"You mean Reid? That's her sister's name," Paul said.

Paul thought a moment, then shrugged. "Dianne probably went home, so she's not missing now."

"If she didn't go home, but decided to hide out here, she might use her former name. But what if she didn't use Reid?"

"She might use the name she had when she was married before," Paul said.

"Paul, you're too clever! Of course. Poppy mentioned it. Calvin." Then Margaret drew a blank. "If all else fails, I could ask Charlie, but I hate to do that. Let's hope she registered as Dianne Reid, and worry about Charlie later." Margaret was off to the house phone again, and again had no luck. No Dianne Reid. What *was* the husband's name? Larry? Harry?

Finally she had no choice but to call Charles Stark, and hope that he was at home. As the phone rang, she tried to recall what Poppy had said. She concentrated on remembering, and the name was beginning to edge into her mind, but it wasn't quite there yet. Dianne had said his name.

"Stark residence." It was not Lourdes who answered, but another woman, perhaps the housekeeper.

"Mr. Stark, please. Lady Margaret Priam calling."

"He is not in to callers," the woman said.

"If he is there, please tell him I'm calling. It's very important. It's about Mrs. Stark."

"I am Mrs. Stark," the woman said. "What is it you have to say about me?"

Conceivably it was the daring former Mrs. Stark, Zoe, as it certainly wasn't Dianne. "It concerns Dianne," Margaret said.

"That woman has caused poor Charles no end of

trouble," Zoe Stark said. "Right from the start. If you will tell me how he can reach you, I will inform him of your call when he is available."

"Cal!" she said aloud, no doubt startling Zoe. She had suddenly remembered his name. "I'm sorry, I was thinking of something else. Thank you so much," Margaret said, "I am unfortunately not available to Mr. Stark myself." She returned to Paul. "Now we have two former spouses to deal with," she said as she sat down and explained about Zoe. "What on earth is she doing there at the Stark apartment?"

"If you cannot find her previous married name from Charles, you must call Poppy," Paul said, and signaled the waiter to refill his wineglass. "Would you care for something? My mother pays the bill."

"I remember his first name," she said. Margaret thought for a moment, then looked up to lock eyes with the handsome waiter who had been on duty when she and Dianne had had tea here. "White wine," she said, and hesitated only a moment before getting up to follow the waiter, abandoning a mystified Paul.

"Have you recently seen the lady who was here with me the other day in the afternoon?"

"The red-haired one, *bella*. She drink Campari soda."

"That's the one," Margaret said. "Have you seen her?"

"When you were here, milady."

"You know me?"

"The world knows Lady Margaret." The waiter grinned. "The friend of the *principéssa*, who is the godmother of Villa d'Este, and"—he glanced over at Paul—*"il prìncipe."* He sounded a bit disparaging of Paul, but the cat may look at a king and be unimpressed, as the waiter clearly was.

"About Mrs. Stark, it's very important that I locate her." She opened her handbag and extracted a twenty-dollar bill, which she could ill afford. The waiter noticed it.

"Yes, milady. I do see her this evening, but she looks different. The hair . . . She passes the lounge and goes to reception. I do not see her again." He was edging a bit too close to Margaret for her complete comfort. She stepped back a pace.

"Do you know what name she used?"

He was surprised. "She has many names?"

An explanation seemed superfluous. "Look, *il prìncipe* would like you to go to the room-service attendant and ask if anyone asked for Campari to be delivered to a room, Campari and . . ." She had a brainstorm. ". . . and a club sandwich with no-fat mayonnaise. I need the room number and the name. The *principéssa* would be grateful as well for this favor." She slipped the twenty into his hand, and the waiter scurried. He was a young man who grasped how things worked.

She sat with Paul again. "The ex-husband's first name was Cal. Calvin, I think. And the second name . . . Got it! Barry. Cal Barry. I'm sure she's using that name."

The waiter was back after a short delay.

"No one ordered Campari. But the little bars in the suites, they have Campari, so she need not have called room service."

Margaret turned away disappointed.

"But I have here a printout of room-service orders since last evening. It may help you."

Margaret scanned the lengthy printout. Most were orders for breakfasts, and someone had ordered enough snacks and drinks for a large party. That wouldn't be Dianne.

But then she found it. Suite 717 had ordered a club sand-wich, specifying no-fat mayonnaise. Thank goodness for Dianne's calorie consciousness, and her love of a good club sandwich.

"Paul, use your considerable influence to find out who is in suite 717. I think it will be Mrs. Calvin Barry."

He went off to the registration desk without hesitation, and returned smiling. His considerable influence appeared to have worked.

"It was a Mrs. Barry," he said.

"Was?"

"She's checked out. Here less than a day."

Dianne had been here and gone. "Where has she gone?"

"Home? At least one hopes," Paul said. "I am not a detective."

"But if she's gone home to Charlie, she'll encounter the former wife. And if she was there when I called, Zoe would have mentioned it. I said I was calling about Di-anne. What do you suppose Zoe is doing there?"

"Perhaps Charles summoned her in his hour of dis-tress," Paul said. "He wished to have family with him. Even if a man is divorced, the first wife is like family."

"Perhaps. But how awful for Dianne." Margaret imag-ined a new wave of stress for the already stressed-out Di-anne. "She could have stayed with me for a few days, rather than running away."

"But if, as you say, she has been threatened, and her sister has been murdered on the street, she would not wish to put a friend in harm's way," Paul said sensibly.

"Some friend I am. Paul, why don't you ring Charlie to check whether Dianne is safely at home? Maybe Mrs. Stark forgot to mention it to me, but will tell you. You have a gift for charming women. Does she know your mother?"

"It is difficult for me to say who my mother knows. The simple answer is 'everyone.' All right, I will call."

Margaret sat alone in the Villa d'Este lounge and sipped her white wine. Suddenly she was aware of the waiter hovering behind her chair. "Yes?"

"About Mrs. Stark," he said. "I didn't mention it before, but another was asking about her today."

"Another what?"

"A man. I had only just come on duty, but he asks all the employees he see about a beautiful red-haired woman, Dianne Stark. I say I do not know her, so he goes away."

"What did he look like, this man?"

"He is very well dressed, and his shoes are very fine. It is the shoes that say how rich a man is, no?"

"I suppose."

"Then, this one is very rich, and very . . ." He waved his hand in front of his face.

"Handsome? *Bello?*"

"I judge that many women would find him so."

"He didn't say his name?" Margaret could not imagine that Gerald Toth, if that's who it was, would state his rather well-known name even to a humble waiter.

"He did not," the waiter said. "Why would he?"

"Then what happened?"

"He went away and spoke to others, and I did not see him again."

"If anyone else comes looking for her, don't say a word. In any event, Mrs. Stark has checked out," Margaret said. The waiter looked interested. "Someone is trying to hurt her. But she is safely gone."

Paul strolled back, frowning.

"Did you speak with Charlie?"

"I did. I asked if Dianne was at home, and he was . . . evasive. I think she is not there, because he asked me if I had seen her today or had made an arrangement to telephone her. He sounded upset."

"Any indication that the other Mrs. Stark was about?"

"None. The telephone was answered by a woman with an accent."

"The nanny." Then she told him what the waiter had said. "I think it must have been Gerald Toth. Do you suppose Dianne arranged to meet him, and now has done a bunk and run off with him?"

Paul looked serious. "I do not see Dianne doing such a thing, do you?"

"No," Margaret said slowly. "She talked about feeling worthless and wanting to return to work, but in the end she said she could not simply abandon Charlie and the baby."

"How can she feel worthless? She is worth a great deal . . ." Paul's face took on that dreamy look he habitually wore when he was thinking about large sums of money.

"Paul," Margaret said sternly. "We are not discussing financial worth. We are talking about self-worth, self-esteem. Dianne's worth as a person."

"She is worth a great deal," Paul repeated firmly. Margaret stood up.

"You're right, she's worth a lot, and we have to do something for her. I know that someone is harassing her, threatening her, and may be close to killing her, so we have to put a stop to it."

"We do? We?"

Margaret sat down again. "Yes. First we'll make a list. I wish I knew her better. It always seems that we all know the same people, have the same experiences and the same feelings and attitudes, but that's not so." She took out a pen and a small notebook and placed them on the table in front of her. "Item: The former husband, Mr. Barry." She wrote carefully. "A threatening letter, an attack on the nanny, calls, anniversary card. No description, except for a tattoo on his arm. Merchant seaman. May be a murderer."

"The former Mrs. Stark?" Paul said helpfully. "She appears suddenly at the Stark home when Dianne goes missing. You say she has been in New York all along. Would she be writing threats, and sending flowers?"

"De Vere did suggest that she might wish to regain her previous lifestyle as Charlie's wife." Margaret wrote down her name. "I'll ask Poppy about Zoe's stability. It seems a bit farfetched, even for an abandoned wife, who in the end did all right for herself. Now we come to the more obvious than Zoe: the admirers. First in line, Gerald Toth. It sounds as though the waiter was describing him as the man who was seeking Dianne earlier today." She hated to think that Gerald had any part in this matter.

"Should we try to contact him?" Paul was uneasy.

"We can't forget Antonio, though. I wouldn't describe him as exceptionally attractive, given to wearing expensive shoes, would you?"

"I don't know that I ever noticed his shoes," Paul said. "I judge him to be attractive to women, at least several years ago. Why shoes?"

"The waiter said that the wealth of a man can be judged by the quality of his shoes."

"True enough," Paul said. "But I don't think that Antonio is rich enough to afford very expensive shoes. Rumor has it that he has to scratch out a living to maintain his lifestyle, relying on illicit cigar sales and the kindness of his lady friends to help him through the bare patches. But I would not be surprised to learn of any bad behavior on his part. Still, a pattern of menacing women is unlike him. I should not think he had a long enough attention span. He might hit them once, and that would be the end of it."

"We have to look at him, though," Margaret said. She glanced at her list. "Barry, Zoe, Gerald, and Antonio. Not many choices."

"Unless Charlie is involved."

"Charlie! What a thought!" Margaret leaned forward. "Why do you have such a thought? And surely he would recognize his own wife immediately and would not shoot her sister by mistake."

Paul squirmed. "If Charlie, for some reason, was discontent in his marriage, he might choose to drive Dianne away, allow her to abandon him and the child, so if they divorced, he would not have to pay out a huge settlement to her."

"Impossible," Margaret said, and as she said it, she almost believed it was possible. Still . . . "Still, if he thought Dianne was encouraging her admirers too much, he might wish to punish her by terrorizing her. But it doesn't sound like the Charlie I know."

"You never know about people, do you?"

"I'll put him on the list," Margaret said, "but I'm not convinced he belongs there. In fact, Dianne said something. No. Impossible."

"What are you thinking?"

"She talked about how much Karen liked the idea of wealth, and that maybe she was a bit too forward with Charlie. I saw her at work myself. Also, the suggestion that the sister had some kind of involvement with the ex-husband. I don't know what it means, because none of that explains the stalking of Dianne."

"Don't forget the servants," Paul said. "Some of these foreigners get strange ideas." He did not appear to recall that Margaret was a "foreigner," and that he himself was half a foreigner.

"In that event, the nanny suddenly becomes an almost active candidate," Margaret said. "She seems to have been involved in some of the happenings—bringing in the anniversary card, the alleged attack in the park. She might have made up her story. That gives us five possibles. I know nothing of the housekeeper, but there is always Reuben, who worked at the building and is rumored to have been fired because of something he did that displeased Dianne."

"And what do we do now?"

"First we try to discover if Dianne has gone off with Gerald Toth."

Margaret hated to admit that she felt a twinge of jealousy. But Gerald wasn't "hers," and she was pretty sure she didn't want him to be. But he was a nice man, and if Dianne was in distress and asked for his help, he would certainly give it, and not care about the gossip that might arise. He was rich enough to buy protection for her if that was necessary, and he seemed to like her enough to want to protect her. On the other hand, if he was behind the threats, seeking his protection was the worst thing Dianne could do.

"I suppose I'll have to ring Gerald or go around to see him," Margaret said. "I'm sure he'll tell me if he's harboring Dianne, especially if I promise I won't tell anyone."

But would he tell her anything, given the play he had made for her on Thursday evening? Might he be reluctant to let her know that he retained an attachment to Dianne while he was trying to attach Margaret? Or if he actually was the person who was harassing Dianne, he certainly wouldn't share her whereabouts.

"Do you know this man well enough to ask?" Paul said. "Aha, I see from your expression that you do know him."

"I met him at a cocktail party just the other day," she said defensively. "We talked about Dianne, and he swore he had nothing to do with annoying her with letters and such. He's quite charming."

"So I understand," Paul said. "Irresistible, in fact. Money does that for a man."

"I didn't find him irresistible," Margaret said, telling a half-truth. "But I do believe he would help a damsel in distress."

"Then, let us find out," Paul said.

"He gave me his address and phone number." She made a show of searching her handbag, although she had put the piece of paper he'd given her away with care. "Here it is. East Seventy-fourth."

"No Park Avenue, no Fifth Avenue for one of the richest men in America?"

"I believe he has modest tastes," Margaret said.

"But I think he may have more elevated tastes when it comes to English titles."

Margaret seldom blushed, but she felt herself blushing now, and knew that Paul had noticed.

"I wonder if De Vere has gone home yet," Margaret said. "I really need to talk to him about all this. Let's ring him."

"Ah," Paul said. "I do detect something happening here. I thought you would ask about Sam the minute you saw me today, but you did not. It required a mention of your involvement with Gerald Toth to cause you to remember De Vere."

"I don't think so," Margaret said, and was quite proud of Paul's perceptiveness.

Chapter 14

*W*hen Dianne did not return promptly, Charles Stark interviewed the doorman who had been on duty the evening of Dianne's disappearance. He had not seen her leaving, but he had noticed a couple of men hanging about outside on the street. "That bum who lives over on Madison on the corner, and some guy I mighta seen before. Youngish, wearing jeans, T-shirt, had a tattoo, like a big dragon. Naw, nobody asked him about Mrs. Stark. She mighta got out without me seeing her. I went to the can for a minute, but one of the building guys was around sweeping."

"Where can I find him?" Charles asked.

"Off duty now, but he woulda told me if he seen one of the tenants leave. That's what he's supposed to do, you know, in case they get a delivery or something. Especially your missus. Miguel thinks the world of her. Always tips him good."

"What about these men you saw?"

"The tattoo guy probably knows your wife. He brought her something a few days back. Say, didn't I just see the other . . . other missus here yesterday?"

"My former wife happened to be in town, and dropped by to visit. She's no longer here. What about this bum?"

"He's kind of a homeless guy, not a bum really. Oh, he panhandles, picks up some spare change. Got a beard, yellow hair. You musta seen him. Northwest corner of Madison. Like it's his permanent address."

Charles Stark set off briskly toward Madison. Night had fallen, and it was cooler than previous days. He hoped the homeless man was at his permanent address.

Dianne Stark huddled in a chair in the unfamiliar bedroom, the lights out and a cup of tea growing cold on the table beside her.

She hadn't known who to turn to when she made the decision to flee. At first the Villa d'Este had seemed like the ideal solution, and she thanked her foresightedness for having kept active one credit card from the days when she was still Dianne Barry. It got her checked into the hotel without a problem, but she knew she couldn't stay there. What if Carolyn Sue had decided to make a trip to New York, and recognized her. Or Margaret might have come looking for her. Margaret was good at solving mysteries, and she'd certainly think of the d'Este. So she'd gotten up the courage to call Gerald, and he had dropped everything to come to her, had convinced her that she would be safe in his guest room, making it clear that there were no strings attached.

Now, for the first time in days, she almost felt safe, unless Gerald was behind the terror. But she believed he could not murder her sister in cold blood. Besides, she felt she had no choice. After Karen's death, she couldn't keep Chip and Charlie in possible danger from some lunatic.

At least she felt heroic, worthwhile. She was doing something to save her family. She was almost tempted to telephone Margaret, not to say where she was, but to have her call Charlie and let him know that she was all right. But then she'd have to tell Margaret her location, and she didn't want to do that.

Somewhere off in the spacious apartment—but far smaller than her own—she heard a telephone ring. Gerald had said he was going out, but he must not have left yet, because the ringing ceased quickly.

A few moments later there was a knock on the door.

"It's me, Gerald," he said. "Margaret seems to have tracked you down to this place. She's coming around shortly."

"I don't want to see her," Dianne said.

"Look, Dianne, you have to. You can't keep running. Open the door, please." She unlocked the door and let him in.

"I'll leave here if I must," she said, and couldn't imagine where she'd go next. Then she said, "I could just become one of the homeless. I know a homeless boy who always hangs around our neighborhood, and he seems to get along quite well. I give him money now and then, and he's told me about the shelters he can go to when it gets cold or rainy. But when it's nice, he just stays out on the street all the time. I think he gets some odd jobs picking up mail to take to the mailbox or delivering packages around the neighborhood. He's nice."

"I don't think you were meant to be homeless," Gerald said. "Margaret told me that you are afraid someone is after you. And your sister's murder is proof of that. I don't think you'd be very safe on the streets."

"My good friend Margaret blabbing about my personal business," Dianne said bitterly.

"That's not fair," Gerald said. "Margaret is very concerned about you. And murder isn't exactly private. Who are you afraid of? Not me, I hope."

"Of course not, but . . . well, you see, I have an ex-husband who probably wants money from me. He can be pretty violent."

"And you've seen him?"

"Not . . . not very often. I know he's around, always around. He sent me an anniversary card just the other day on the date of our wedding, so I know he's around, and he's watching me."

"Then we'll have to get rid of him."

"Gerald!"

"I don't mean it the way it sounded, but we'll get the police on it."

"That's what Margaret said. Her boyfriend is a police-man, and she said he'd help."

Gerald was thoughtful. "I see. Well, naturally a pretty woman like Margaret would have a beau. Here, let me get you a fresh cup of tea."

"If you don't mind," Dianne said, "I'd like a Campari and soda. If you have any."

Gerald thought for a minute. "I don't, I'm afraid. But I can run around the corner and buy some for you. It won't take more than five minutes."

"You're too good, Gerald," she said, and as soon as the door closed behind him, she repacked the few things she'd taken from her small overnight bag, gathered up her handbag, put on her shoes, and was ready to leave.

Charles Stark was not gone long from his apartment, and when he returned, he listened to the message left on the an-swering machine. It was Margaret, telling him that Dianne had been located, and was safe. Another call would follow as soon as she had more news.

Charles wasn't feeling well, but he went to the kitchen to see what the housekeeper had left in the refrigerator. He was hungry, since he hadn't been able to eat since Dianne's disappearance. He could hear the television in Lourdes's room, a snappy jingle urging viewers to buy some sort of automobile.

He carried a dish of ice cream into the master bedroom he had shared with Dianne before she decided that he would sleep better if she took one of the guest rooms. Having Karen here had been a nice diversion for her, although Dianne had been grumpy because he didn't hesitate to give Karen a few dollars here and there so she would enjoy New York. Karen had even asked him if he could find her a job at his company. . . . But in the end, Charlie wasn't sure how Dianne felt about her sister. A lot of sibling rivalry there, if he wasn't mistaken. She'd behaved oddly about Karen's death when she'd gotten over the immediate shock of it. Almost relieved that she was gone.

Wherever she decided to sleep, Dianne still kept all of her possessions in the master bedroom, and he started to look through the drawers. Finally he came upon the letter that stated the writer's intention of killing his wife, and he felt strangely better. At least he knew that she hadn't been imagining things, and that Karen's murder had surely been a case of mistaken identity. He probably should have demanded that Margaret tell him where Dianne was, but it didn't seem important now. She'd be home soon enough, likely still complaining about how useless her life was. He did not understand why she just couldn't relax and enjoy the life he provided for her and Chip.

Charlie spent a good hour pacing about the apartment, heard Chip start to cry, heard Lourdes shuffle from her room to soothe him. Then silence. Margaret didn't call again, and Dianne didn't come through the door. He heard sirens outside on the cross street, but paid them no heed. Finally, he went to bed, leaving lights on all over the apartment.

Dianne Stark found a taxi quickly outside Gerald's building. In fact, she saw his back as he rounded the corner on his way to buy Campari for her, but he didn't look back, and she ducked down as the cab passed the corner, just in case he lingered there and caught sight of her.

"La Guardia Airport," she told the driver. "Take the bridge."

She liked the view of the city from the Fifty-ninth Street Bridge, the jagged row of sparkling high-rises on the Manhattan side and the green thrust of the tall, new Citicorp Building in Queens towering above the dark, low factories and residential buildings. She remembered that somewhere in their midst, Carolyn Sue had developed a housing complex. In the distance she could see the Manhattan and Brooklyn Bridges spanning the East River.

Traffic was not heavy, and they soon reached the turnoff for the airport.

"What airline, lady?"

She named the airline she'd once worked for. It was too much to hope that she'd see the familiar face of one of her old colleagues, and maybe that wouldn't be such a good idea. At least she had an old, official-looking ID with her picture and her former married name, so it would match the name on the ticket she would buy with her old credit card. She hoped she could pass security without any problems with the ID.

Before she bought her ticket to Dallas, she called Carolyn Sue.

"It's Dianne Stark, Carolyn Sue, and I need your help desperately," she said. "I'm running away from home. Please don't tell Charlie or Margaret or anybody, but can I stay with you for a few days?"

"Why, you sure can, honey. What's the problem? Charlie beatin' up on you?"

"Nothing like that." She hesitated to mention Karen's murder and her stalker. "I just need to get away."

"I'll send a car to meet you. What flight you goin' to be on?"

Dianne had already checked the departures screen and seen that a flight was leaving in forty-five minutes, arriving at Dallas/Fort Worth Airport near midnight. "I haven't bought the ticket yet, but I should be in at eleven fifty-four. If the plane is full, I'll book another flight and call you."

"I don't know that I feel quite right about harboring a runaway," Carolyn Sue said, "but what the hell. You got to do something interesting with your life."

"How true," Dianne said.

Chapter 15

"*She's scampered again,*" Gerald said when Margaret arrived at his place in a rush. "I left her for five minutes, no more, and she left. Took all her things with her. Now what do we do?"

Margaret collapsed into a chair. "I don't know. And I told Charlie she was okay. Oh, I didn't say where she was, just that she was safe. If she came to you, do you suppose she could have decided to go to Antonio?"

"I hope not," Gerald said. "He's real lowlife. I wouldn't put threats past him, either. But from what Dianne told me, I don't think she had any interest at all in him, and I doubt seriously that she would put her life in his hands."

"I wish we could locate this ex-husband of hers."

"That's more a job for your policeman friend," Gerald said coolly.

"Sam's busy, and he's already told me that there's not much the police can do except to keep investigating the murder. I mean, if there was proof that she'd actually been kidnapped or harmed in some way . . . How do you know about Sam?" She had managed to find De Vere at home, and he had promised that he would be free to see her tomorrow.

133

"Gossip," Gerald said. "But I intend to compete very actively for your affections."

Margaret put her face in her hands. "Compete if you must, but I'd rather know what's become of Dianne. She has money and a credit card, in her former name, so she can check into any hotel she chooses."

"Or travel anywhere she chooses. She used to be a flight attendant, right?" Margaret nodded. "Then, I assume she would think first of flying somewhere."

"But where? And we can't ask every airline in the greater New York area if a Dianne Barry booked a flight with them."

"But she would probably think first of her old airline, would she not? Do you know which one it was?"

Margaret did, and Gerald placed a call to someone he said "could handle things." Then he offered her a Campari and soda from the stock he'd bought for Dianne. "He'll be able to get the information if she took a flight. I use him to find out things for me all the time, and he's good."

As they waited for a return call, Gerald talked some more about his life, the wonderful house he owned in Marin, the pleasures of San Francisco, visits to the wine country, Monterey, and Big Sur. It sounded peaceful and joyous, and Margaret slipped into a doze, only to be startled awake by the phone.

"We got her," Gerald said as he hung up. "She booked a flight to Dallas, of all places. It just took off. Why would she do that?"

"She has friends everywhere," Margaret said. "I guess Dallas is as safe as anyplace, and goodness knows, Carolyn Sue is probably well armed." She explained about Paul's mother.

"I do happen to know her. Benton Hoopes and I had some business dealings a few years ago."

"I never thought of Ben as a computer person," Margaret said.

"He tends to be around when there's money to be made," Gerald said. "Just as I am. I do have interests outside of computers." He smiled at her, and again she felt the magnetism he could generate with just a look.

"Now that we've located Dianne, I should call Charlie and then be getting home."

"You needn't leave," he said.

"Yes," Margaret said, "yes, I do need to leave."

When she arrived home, she called Paul, hoping that De Vere would answer, but it was the Prince who picked up the phone. "Home already?" she asked. "I thought you always went out on a Saturday night."

"I do, but I haven't left yet. Things do not happen early in New York, especially on Saturday nights."

"I would like a favor, please. Call your mother and find out whether Dianne is coming to her and when she is arriving. Then tell me. You can promise Carolyn Sue that neither you nor I will tell anyone where Dianne is."

"But you could easily call my mother . . . What is this about?"

"Dianne has very cleverly gone to Dallas, and I suspect she's making for Carolyn Sue who has sworn not to tell anyone, but you can get around her. She dotes on you, even if she isn't as openhanded as you might wish. Please."

"I will do it." Paul sounded as though he knew his reluctance would be overcome even if he argued for an hour.

"I don't suppose you've heard from De Vere."

"Nothing more than what I told you earlier. He's out detecting."

"He promised to call me tomorrow." She felt a strong need to hear his voice.

"Then, he will. I will call you as soon as I have spoken with my mother."

Not five minutes later, the phone rang.

"Dianne will be in Dallas around midnight," Paul said. "I told my mother about her troubles and told her to keep her safe. But no one will follow her there, do you think?"

"If I had no trouble figuring out that she took flight on her old airline, perhaps Mr. Barry will think of it. Although I doubt that he has the influence Gerald has to determine where she went or the money to follow her."

"Gerald? You seem to be in frequent contact with him," Paul said.

"We're working together on Dianne's problem."

"At least it does not involve a murder," Paul said. "De Vere would not like that."

"But it already does involve a murder. I just hope there will not be another one." Paul promised to keep in touch. As soon as she had hung up, the phone rang again.

"Margaret? Charles Stark here." His voice on the phone sounded fuzzy. "Any news of Dianne?"

"Ah . . . she's staying with a friend, someone I know well and trust. She's out of harm's way."

"Did you know she was threatened even before this thing with Karen?"

"So I understood. I thought you knew. But Mr. Barry won't be able to find her."

"Barry? What's he got to do with it?"

"I . . . she assumed that it was he who was annoying her, probably to get money from you."

"Hmmm, possible. But surely he's out at sea."

"He's been seen, or at least we believe it was he."

"And what did he look like?"

"I have no idea, we just put some facts together, and made some assumptions. It has to be him."

"I see. If you speak with Dianne, please ask her to call me, to come home. Chip misses her. I miss her. It will be all right now. She'll be safe, or will be if we can lure him out into the light and face up to him."

Margaret thought for a moment. What she thought of was completely foolhardy and terribly dangerous. "Charlie, I have an idea. If Dianne's stalker is lurking around your building, we might be able to get him to approach Dianne . . ."

"I won't allow it."

"What I meant was, I know I don't look as much like her as Karen did, but we're about the same height. I could get my hair cut and curled. I'd wear sunglasses and some concealing garment that wouldn't shout that I'm not as svelte as the real thing. I could go in and out of the building, maybe pushing Chip in his stroller—with Edgardo following on my heels for protection—and he might try to approach me. If he does anything dangerous, we'll have him arrested."

Charlie said firmly, "Margaret, you realize that if he was able to walk up to Karen and shoot her, then he just as easily could walk up to you and do the same. I won't allow it. And I won't allow Chip to be bait for a maniac."

"All right, then, we'll stuff some blankets in the stroller and just pretend that he's sitting there."

"I don't know," Charlie said slowly. "What does De Vere have to say about this?"

"He hasn't objected," Margaret said. She didn't like to

tell lies, but this was serious business. Of course De Vere would forbid her to do such a thing.

"I wouldn't want you to go strolling in the park, even with Edgardo nearby. And you'd have to stay here, to be able to go in and out on a regular schedule. Can you come around tonight? I'll have Lourdes fix up a guest room for you. Lourdes will welcome a solution to this mess. The murder and that attack the other day scared her silly. When you get here, we'll have to figure out how to get the doormen to join in the masquerade. Money will do that. And Margaret, please don't feel you have to change your hair. You can wear a hat. Dianne has several of those floppy things she often wears to keep the sun off her face."

"I'll be around in half an hour," Margaret said. "We'll lick this together."

Margaret tossed a few things in a bag, and was glad that the spring days were somewhat cool. It was hard to disguise oneself in light summer frocks. Better a sudden cold spell. And she was relieved that Charlie halted her plan to change her hair. If it weren't so late, she could have bought a wig. That was something to think about tomorrow. She'd have to plan carefully. Did Dianne regularly wear slacks? Well, everybody did, and they were a necessity for the disguise, since Margaret's legs, although shapely enough, were scarcely as slim as Dianne's. At least she would not be required to don a bias-cut satin evening gown, Dianne's favorite dress-up garb, but definitely not suited to Margaret. I should have joined that health club long ago, she thought.

Her last act was to put Elinor's envelopes in a shopping bag so that she could address them at the Stark apartment while she entertained little Chip.

She descended to her lobby, and informed the doorman

that she'd be gone a few days. He should take in any packages for her, and if her mailbox started to overflow, he could bundle up the mail and keep it for her.

"I may pass by to pick up the mail, though," she said. "And if anyone comes looking for me, give out this number." She scrawled the Starks' number on a card, and handed it to him.

"Okay, Lady Margaret. Will do."

She decided to walk to the Starks' apartment. It was getting dark, and it was cooler than it had been, but she thought her arrival might be less noticeable to a watcher if she didn't emerge from a cab, but came on foot.

She took the same route as she had the other day, but the shopwindows were dark and the students were probably all at their desks studying for final exams.

At the corner of Madison and the Starks' cross street, she saw the homeless man. He appeared to be sleeping, leaning against the building, but he spoke as she passed him.

"Hello, lady," he said. "I didn't thank you enough for getting the cops off my back the other day. You shouldn't be walking around alone at night with some guy out here shooting people."

"I'm almost where I'm going," Margaret said. She pulled a dollar bill from her pocket and dropped it in his empty coffee container.

"Thanks," he said. "I could walk down the street with you, sort of protect you."

She hesitated. He seemed harmless enough. "It's just a few buildings along. I'll be all right." But the man had gotten to his feet and was fluffing his beard and straightening his clothes.

"You English?"

"Actually, I am. But I've lived in New York for several years."

"My name's John," he said. "I was in England once when I was in the navy. You meet a lot of navy guys in my line of work."

Panhandling didn't seem to Margaret to be the most fulfilling of work, but if he thought so, so be it. "I'm Margaret," she said. "I say. I'm going to be staying on this street for a time."

"So we'll be like neighbors."

"Yes, but the thing is, I don't want you to recognize me if you see me. I have to pretend to be someone else."

"You like an actress?" They were very near the building now.

"Something like that. Please don't call me Margaret. Call me Dianne, if you say a name at all."

John looked at her suspiciously. "What kind of scam are you working?"

"It's not a scam, but it's . . . it's impossible to explain. It has something to do with the woman who got shot. I asked you this before, but have you seen the man who hangs about this building, and probably did the shooting? Ordinary-looking, jeans and T-shirt, but he has a tattoo on one arm. He's a merchant seaman. You said you'd seen someone like that."

"Cal, I think he calls himself something like that. Yeah, he's around a lot, like I said. The cops were looking for him after the shooting. Cheap son of a bitch. Gave me a dime once like it was a million bucks, and I should be down on my knees thanking him. I got the idea he was a private eye, spying on some rich man who's running around on his wife. He's a weird guy, talks to himself, and stares up at the building like he's watching a movie. I asked him what he was doing, and he told me to get lost. Mean."

"John, I'm going to take you into my confidence. Your friend Cal is trying to frighten a lady who lives here. The one whose sister was shot. I think whoever did it was trying to shoot my friend. You may have seen her, very pretty, with curly red hair . . . well, it's blond now."

"Sure, I know the one you mean. Has a cute little kid that the Chinese lady takes for walks. Gives me change every now and then, and she even gave me a ten at Christmas. This guy's after her?"

"We believe he's her former husband, and he's threatened to kill her. He managed to get her sister, so now Dianne's gone away to hide from him, and I'm going to pretend to be her for a few days, to see if we can get him to show himself."

John shook his head. "That's plain stupid, lady. He's going to kill you next. You know, I'm thinking being rich isn't all it's cracked up to be. You take a guy like me, living on the street, begging for a little money to buy a sandwich and a coffee, and I got no problems at all compared to this lady, who's got a nut stalking her. Makes you think. Okay, lady. I don't know you. You take care now." He started to walk away, then turned back. "But remember, old John'll be at his corner keeping an eye on you."

Chapter 16

The doorman announced her, and Lourdes was at the door to greet her. She did look a bit Chinese.

"We are so happy you will be here," Lourdes said. "I think maybe Chip will think you're almost his mother, and you can read to him and show him pictures. He doesn't like me to read. Come this way to your room. Mr. Stark has retired." She looked at Margaret shyly. "Mr. Stark has told me of your plan, and I will help if I can. So Mrs. Stark can come home, and maybe we can find who shoot the nice Miss Reid." Lourdes looked tearful.

"Lourdes, have you ever seen the man we believe shot Miss Reid and is trying to harm Mrs. Stark?"

She shrugged. "There is one who seems to often be on the street. But he never bothers me."

"But is he the one who attacked you when you were walking Chip?"

She shook her head. "It happened so fast, and I was frightened. But it could have been him. Maybe Edgardo saw him."

"Lourdes, were there many times when someone tried to get to Mrs. Stark? Letters, and such? Not just that card that the man left."

Lourdes hung her head. "She tried to hide it from me

142

and Mr. Stark. He did not know how often it happened . . . The phone calls all the time, and the man would say terrible things."

"Such as?"

"He would find her, she would not escape him. Even that he would hurt her if she did not come to the park to meet him. Then she told me never to answer the phone, to have the answering machine answer. But he still left messages. She would erase them as soon as she heard them. She said she saw him standing across the street when she looked from the windows and when she went out. He knew when she was going to her flower class, so she stopped going. I was frightened all the time. I still am. He could be out there on the street, waiting for me. Or you now. I think he will be angry if he finds that you are trying to fool him by pretending to be Mrs. Stark."

"Don't worry. We'll manage quite well," Margaret said.

"This man is the one she was married to, is he not? She spoke of him to me, when the calls started coming all the time."

"It appears that it is Mr. Barry, her ex-husband, although we don't know for certain."

"I don't know what to do," Lourdes said.

"I have a friend who is a policeman," Margaret said. "He will help us."

"If you say it will be well," Lourdes said. She did not sound convinced. "Come now to your room. The housekeeper will be here at seven in the morning. Mr. Stark asked her to come in, even if it is Sunday. I will tell her that you are here, and she will prepare your breakfast."

"But don't tell her exactly why I'm here. She might gossip with the building staff, and I don't want everybody knowing our plan. Mr. Barry might learn of it before we're ready."

"I will say only that you are a friend of Mrs. Stark's awaiting her return."

The guest bedroom was beautifully comfortable, with a canopied bed made up with sheets that felt like silk and a pile of plump, down-filled pillows. There was a little television set placed for easy viewing and a huge dressing table with flattering lights. Margaret unpacked her few things, and got into bed. Then she worried a long time about whether she would be able to carry out the plan to impersonate Dianne and draw Barry out. Was it even wise or just extremely foolhardy? She knew the answer to that, even without De Vere or Paul around to tell her so, but it was the only plan she could think of. She wished De Vere were around to counsel her.

He certainly would refuse to allow her to carry out the plan, but if she managed to get around that minor impediment, he would have good advice on how to go about doing it. Then she wondered if she should consult with Paul. He'd be opposed, too, but it would be comforting to have someone on her side other than an upset Charlie. She eyed the white telephone and shook her head. By now Paul would be out at a club, wooing some pretty young thing. She had no doubt that he would not consider a brief dalliance any betrayal of the Honorable Georgina.

So she telephoned De Vere, and no one answered. She left the Starks' phone number, asking for a call tomorrow.

Margaret snuggled under the princely sheets and tried to sleep. It was no good. Her mind was racing, imagining the terrors that Dianne had been subjected to by her stalker, even feeling the emptiness and pointlessness of the kind of life they both were leading. All she had to do herself was address those invitations for Elinor.

Then she thought about Gerald. He had made a definite impression on her, and she wondered if she was betraying De Vere. Still, if she needed Gerald as backup for her coming adventure, he would surely be there for her. Gradually Margaret drifted into sleep.

High above the state of Texas, the announcement was made that the plane carrying Dianne Stark/aka Dianne Barry was beginning its descent and would be landing at the Dallas/Fort Worth Airport in twenty minutes.

Dianne stirred from her doze. The plane was nearly empty, and the cabin crew was moving about, leisurely picking up empty plastic tumblers and cold cups of coffee in preparation for landing. She had not seen anyone she knew from the old days, although the pilot's name was familiar. She was sure she'd flown with him numerous times, but they had never had more than a nodding acquaintance. She was safe, for the moment. She was someplace where no one could find her. No committee chairlady, no Gerald, no Calvin Barry.

She still had no idea why Cal was trying to make her life miserable by threats. Even the times when he wrote that he still loved her, she felt threatened. If it was money he wanted, why didn't he come right out and ask for it? She'd never done anything to hurt him. Except to leave him. And that was a decision with which he had concurred. At the time. She knew he had girls in some of his ports, if not all, and when she was flying across the United States or to Europe, he was at sea for months. They seldom spent more than a few weeks a year together in their shabby little house near Providence.

Of course, he was resentful if she had to fly for a few days while he was home, but wasn't he away much more often than she? He'd wanted her to have a child, so that she would always be at home, but they needed her income. She needed her income because, even before Charlie's wealth was at her disposal, she liked pretty clothes and expensive shoes. Her mother never cared for him, but Mom never interfered in their marriage, so that mild antagonism could scarcely be the reason for his present unwelcome attentions. Mother had died nearly eight years ago, in any case, right after the divorce. Then there was Karen, who always claimed that Cal was "cute." So cute that Dianne was sure she'd had an affair with him, and that had caused major friction in their marriage. Not that Karen had cared. She claimed free-spirit status, with free meaning she could do what she wanted and damn the consequences.

Cal had never understood why Dianne was so upset about him and Karen. Well, Karen had gotten what she deserved, even if she'd only spent a little of Charlie's money.

The FASTEN SEAT BELTS sign flashed on, and the few people on the plane stirred, putting their seats upright and closing their tray tables. Although she was sitting on the aisle, there was no one else in her row, so Dianne could lean and catch a glimpse of scattered lights on the ground below. The cabin crew had taken seats and fastened themselves in, and she heard the rumble of the landing gear. The pilot made a smooth landing and taxied to the terminal. Now that she was in Dallas, Dianne felt a small clutch of apprehension, unsure how Carolyn Sue would view her dilemma.

The man who met her was wearing a chauffeur's uniform, but he looked like a cowboy, with tanned face and eyes that appeared to be narrowed by looking too much at the sun-drenched prairies. "Mrs. Stark? Right this way." He guided her through the airport out to the roadway. "Now, you wait right here, and I'll bring the car around, unless you want to walk to the garage."

It was hot in Dallas, but not unpleasant. "I'll wait. I've been shut up in the plane, and the night air is nice."

The driver loped off, and Dianne stood at the curbside, watching arriving passengers greeting loved ones and driving away. There didn't seem to be a lot of outgoing traffic, but, of course, it was close to midnight. Mostly international flights going out at this hour.

The driver was soon back in a long white Lincoln that was air-conditioned, but smelled faintly of Carolyn Sue's signature perfume. "Mrs. Hoopes planned to meet you," the driver said, "but she got on the phone with her son, and told me to go along by myself. She said to say she'd be waiting for you at the house. It's gonna take us half an hour, so you just lean back and relax."

They sped along the freeway toward the city, past flat fields and occasional office parks that were clusters of buildings made of reflecting glass, past vast car dealerships and fast-food restaurants. The driver was blessedly silent, although Dianne could hear, very faintly, the sounds of country music from the front seat.

Dianne had never visited Carolyn Sue's home, but Paul had once called it "obscenely large," and had indicated that his mother's closets were bigger than most New York City apartments. The car had turned off the freeway onto a comparatively unpopulated road. There were a few lights in the distance, as if settlers had built their little homes in the depths of the prairie.

"The ranch is just a few miles along here," the driver said suddenly.

"A real ranch? I had no idea."

"Well, now. They have a few head of cattle, and horses an' stuff. Not that they do any real ranchin' here. They got a real big spread farther south. They just call this the ranch so's they can have an excuse for a big place away from the city and other folks. And they got room for the helicopter pad in case Mr. Hoopes has to get someplace fast. You ain't gonna find lots of cowboys and the like. But it's a real impressive place."

Which was an understatement. They turned into a drive that went on for a mile or two. It was lined with lighted lampposts every few hundred feet and a white fence on either side. Finally the drive rose up gently to the top of a little hill, and Dianne could look down in the distance at a house approximately the size of the Pentagon. It was hard to see it clearly in the darkness, but it was white, and the drive ended in front of a pillared portico ablaze with lights. A butler was taking her bag from the car almost before it had come to a complete stop, and was guiding her into the house, where she faced a magnificent foyer that seemed to house any number of crystal lighting fixtures and huge mirrors.

"This way, ma'am. Mrs. Hoopes is in the white drawing room." The butler wasn't English; in fact, he appeared to be Mexican, but he was striving for a clipped semi-English accent. The white drawing room was very white indeed. Blindingly white. White carpet, white drapes, white overstuffed furniture, white roses in white vases, even a white grandfather clock. A glass étagère was crammed with white porcelain figurines. And there on a sofa (white) was Carolyn Sue, white blond hair, and wearing white jeans and boots and a white fringed leather jacket. At least the room was cool enough to support her outfit.

"Dianne, darlin', you look all done in. Set right down and tell me your sad, sad tale. Mr. Sanchez will be bringing us somethin' nice and cold to drink."

"I could use iced tea, lots of ice," Dianne said, although she was certain Carolyn Sue's mansion was well stocked with anything she might desire. No running to the corner shop for Campari in this establishment. She felt a sudden pang of guilt about running off from Gerald's place without a word. He must be frantic, but not more than poor Charlie. And Margaret, if she'd heard Dianne had disappeared again.

The butler bowed slightly and bustled away.

"I suppose I ought to tell people where I am," Dianne said reluctantly.

"Not to worry," Carolyn Sue said. "Simply everybody knows."

Chapter 17

To Margaret's relief, the new day started out cloudy with showers. The Starks' housekeeper, a hefty, stern individual, brought her tea and toast and looked disapproving.

"I only take orders from Mr. Stark," she said. "My name is Lucille, and I don't usually work on Sundays. I'm just helping out while Mrs. Stark is away. I leave at noon today, but there will be something in the refrigerator for luncheon. Mr. Stark said there was no need to prepare dinner."

"Thank you, Lucille. I don't need anything, and I'll only be here a day or two. Mrs. Stark should be back shortly." Margaret wondered if Lucille was imagining some kind of hanky-panky between her and Charlie. She put Lucille and her suspicions out of her mind and considered her next step.

If she was to show herself to Barry on the street, she could logically wear a trench coat and hat for her impersonation of Dianne, although sunglasses were probably a bit too much for a damp, cloudy day. She donned slacks and sneakers and pinned up her blond hair—longer than Dianne's—to hide under the hat. Lourdes found her an umbrella, and she put on Dianne's coat. It was pinkish and waterproof, and Lourdes told her that Dianne always wore it when she went for a walk on cool days. The coat would help foster the illusion of Dianne. Then she tied a pale blue scarf around her neck. Lourdes said Dianne often wore it. In fact, Lourdes was taking almost too much pleasure in the charade. Margaret supposed it beat listening to Chipper's baby songs over and over and over.

"I'm going to walk over to Madison," she told Lourdes. Charlie remained unseen in his room. "If I am not back in an hour, call this number and tell the young man that I am missing." She gave her Paul's number. He would be sleeping in after a late night on the town, but he could jolly well get up to rescue her, or get De Vere to do it. She'd rather be rescued by De Vere, even with the tongue-lashing she would be sure to get for trying this stunt. "Don't take Chip for a walk today."

"I would not take Chip out while the weather is bad," Lourdes said.

Feeling inadequately disguised, Margaret went down to the lobby and peered out onto the damp street. There were no suspicious lurkers to be seen. She pulled the hat brim down over her face and stepped bravely from the building, then quickly raised the umbrella. She walked slowly and carefully in the direction of Madison Avenue. One or two dog walkers, out early on a Sunday morning, passed her coming from the opposite direction, and an occasional car drove by. Altogether, it was an uneventful stroll. John was not at his usual post on the corner, the rain perhaps having driven him to seek shelter off the street. Suddenly Margaret sensed someone approaching her from behind, and she tensed. She kept her head down, with the open umbrella close to hide her face, but it was just an elderly man leaning on a cane, doing his best to hurry along.

At Madison she turned downtown and walked a few blocks, feeling the cool mist of a light rain blowing in her face. She turned right onto a cross street until she again reached Fifth Avenue, and turned uptown to return to the Starks' building. There were more people here, walking on the opposite side of Fifth along the stone wall that marked the edge of the park. She scanned them surreptitiously, paying heed only to one man wearing a windbreaker and leaning against the wall. He was exactly opposite the Starks' apartment building, and when she turned in toward the building's entrance, he seemed to straighten up and watch her.

I think you're imagining things, she thought, but allowed herself a backward look. He was still there, and she was sure he was still watching her. Then, strolling down the street in her direction, she saw John. He grinned at her.

"You playacting today?"

"A little bit. I needed some air."

He looked beyond her. "I think I'm seeing the guy I told you about, across Fifth. Cheap Calvin, the one who hangs around here."

"Really? Look, I don't want him to see me talking to you. It could get you in trouble."

"Lady, I can take care of myself. Say, you have any spare change you could give me? I need to get something to eat. An' if he sees you giving me a handout, he won't think another thing about it. Mrs. Stark used to pass me spare change anyhow."

"I didn't bring anything . . . Wait." She felt in the pocket of her slacks and found a dollar bill. "Here, it's all I have with me."

"That's okay," John said. "You better go inside now."

"Why?"

" 'Cause that guy's coming across the street in your direction. Maybe he still got that gun."

"Thanks," she said. "Remember, don't say anything. Or if he asks anything, you tell him I'm Mrs. Stark. Dianne."

"Whatever. You take care, now."

Margaret hurried into the building, feeling a little shaky at her almost close encounter with Cal Barry, and spent the rest of the morning addressing envelopes for the invitations. Charlie did not show himself, and when she joined Lourdes to play with Chip for a few minutes, Lourdes told her that Mr. Stark had gone out, saying he wouldn't return until the evening.

Chip appeared to enjoy Margaret's attentions. Remembering what Dianne had said about reading, she spent some time reciting lines from a book about giving a cookie to a mouse. Chip's reaction was to fall promptly asleep.

"He likes that story," Lourdes said, "but he didn't sleep good last night. He misses his momma."

Margaret glanced at her watch. It would only be ten o'clock in Dallas, perhaps too early to telephone Dianne to see if she was safely under Carolyn Sue's control.

"I may go out again," she said with no firm idea about where she might go. "Or make a few phone calls." Maybe De Vere had tried to call her. But no, he had the Starks' number, but then, he might have tried to call from the precinct. She could check her machine messages from here. He might have left a number for her to call. Or she could walk to her apartment and listen to her messages in person.

"I will stay here and write to my daughter in the Philippines," Lourdes said, "and when Chip wakes, I will give him his lunch. If the weather has cleared, we will go for a walk."

"No!" Margaret said quickly, startling Lourdes. "I mean, I think it would not be a good idea to go out with Chip today."

Lourdes nodded, but did not appear to be convinced.

"I will be back early this afternoon," Margaret said. "We'll decide then about the walk." If anybody was going to walk Chip, it was going to be Margaret.

The skies were beginning to clear, so when she reassumed her Dianne disguise, she wore sunglasses, but decided to take the umbrella as well.

This time when she peered out from the lobby, she saw the same man across the street. She felt a tingle of anticipation, but not fear, not yet. She approached the doorman, who was leaning on his desk, apparently fascinated by the static scenes showing on the little TV monitors from the security cameras.

"Excuse me. There's a man standing across the street. I wonder if you've seen him around here before. Oh, please, don't let him think you're checking on him. I don't want him to know . . ."

"I understand," the doorman said, and casually opened the door and looked up as if checking on the weather. He picked up a scrap of paper sullying the wide mat in front of the door and returned to his post.

"I've seen him lots of times," he said. "Doesn't do anything, just stands there. I figure he's one of these bums looking for a handout."

"Or maybe he's the guy who shot Karen Reid," Margaret prodded. The doorman straightened up and looked serious. "Does he ever ask anyone for money?"

The doorman thought about that. "Come to think about

it, I never seen him panhandle. But, like, I can't call the cops just because a guy's standing around. Besides, I don't think he's the one who did the shooting. Anyhow, there was a cop here for a day after the shooting, but he's gone now. They checked him out and musta decided he wasn't involved."

"Has he ever spoken to you? About people in this building?"

"Guy's never said a word to me. But if he'd asked about any of the tenants, then I would call the cops. Sorry."

"It's okay. But maybe you should call the cops anyhow. I'm going out now. Could you keep watch and see if he follows me?"

"Sure. What do I do if he does?"

"Nothing. I'm just curious."

Margaret again pulled the floppy brim of her hat down to hide her face, stepped briskly out onto the sidewalk, and walked purposefully down the street. This time she did find John at the corner of Madison, and paused briefly to hand him another dollar and to whisper, "See if the man from the park is following me."

Then she continued on without looking back until she reached her own building.

"They said you were away," her doorman said.

"I forgot something, but if anyone asks for me, I'm not here." She managed to look back over her shoulder, and for a brief moment was almost certain she saw the man from the Starks' building passing the doorway. He surely saw her talking to the doorman, so she hoped he would think that Dianne was visiting her friend.

She hurried up to her apartment, and noticed that she had a message on her machine. Before she had a chance to listen to it, however, the phone began to ring. She waited until the machine message started, "Hello," she heard her voice say, "you've reached . . ." the number, the fact that no one could take the call now, please leave a message. She was poised to pick up if she heard De Vere's voice; however, it was not Sam who spoke, but another man.

"I know where you are, Dianne, and I'll be waiting for you when you come back. You tell her that, Lady What's-it. You can't hide Dianne. She belongs to me." Click, and he was gone. Margaret felt trembly inside just from the very thought that the man had followed her, and knew who Margaret was, even if he had been fooled by her impersonation. But had he? She listened to the message again, and made sure to save it. She was to *tell* Dianne. Almost as though he knew Dianne was not here. He'd be there when she came *back*. Almost as though he knew she was away. But how could he know Dianne wasn't in town? Very puzzling and unnerving.

She listened to her other messsages, and was not surprised to hear from Gerald, wanting to know if everything had worked out for Dianne, from Paul, who was also worried, and finally from De Vere, who sounded relaxed and unconcerned. Well, he didn't know what was happening. And he left assurances that if she called him late this afternoon, he would be there. She wanted him there right now.

First off, she called Paul. He sounded as though he were still half asleep. "I assume Dianne reached your mother safely," she said.

"She did. My mother called far too early this morning. I think that Dianne must have told her all about the problem, because Carolyn Sue sounded well-informed. She says she will not allow her to leave until De Vere tells her it is safe to do so. I told her that De Vere was not involved in the matter, but she trusts only him."

"Paul, listen. I pretended to be Dianne today, and someone followed me. He actually left a message on my answering machine. At first I thought he believed she was with me, but now I'm not so sure. It was a somewhat threatening message."

"Margaret, I do not care for this kind of business," Paul said. "It sounds very dangerous. Should I rush to protect you?"

"Thank you, but no. If Mr. Barry is convinced that Dianne is away, he won't trouble me. He'll wait for her to come back, which she must do eventually. That's why we must stop him."

"But he will be angry that you have misled him," Paul said. "Margaret, he could walk up and shoot you. Please take taxis, and do not walk about the streets alone."

"I promise," Margaret said. Then she rang Gerald, who was pleased to know that Dianne had reached Dallas. He wanted to see Margaret that evening. He wanted to be sure they were still dining out tomorrow. He wanted to know if there were any plays she wanted to see, places she wanted to visit. He would even arrange to fly her to Dallas.

Margaret thought that if she stated that she wanted multi-carat diamond earrings, he would arrange to have them delivered before sundown. Immense wealth was very seductive.

Chapter 18

M*argaret* remained in her apartment, reluctant to return to a tedious afternoon with Lourdes and Chip at the Starks' apartment, and maybe just a little frightened to show herself on the street. Here at least she could write a letter or two, and eat a bit of lunch, and yes, finally call Dianne in Texas.

"Margaret, darlin'!" Carolyn Sue sounded overjoyed to hear her voice. "We're makin' out just fine. But poor Dianne is like a wilted little flower. She's told me all about her poor sister and that beastly man who was following her around until she ran away."

"He's still following her," Margaret said, "or thinks he is, but it's only me." Margaret told her about her plan to attempt to impersonate Dianne.

"Isn't that dangerous? She said he was not a gentle man, but," she added softly, "from what she's been telling me, I'm not so sure she's got him completely out of her system. Anyhow, I can't have you doin' this, Margaret honey."

"Paul has offered to protect me, but I didn't want to involve him."

"Well, he sure would offer to protect you. I raised my boy to have courage. You take care, now, and you have my permission to involve Paul as much as you want, although I'd hate to see my precious boy damaged. Where's Sam?"

"He's busy today until this afternoon. I don't want to involve him, either. He'll just be cross with me."

"Well, he can handle danger. He's a policeman."

"And for that very reason, he'd forbid me to proceed. I want to draw this ex-husband out of the shadows."

"And do what?" Carolyn Sue asked sensibly. Indeed, what did Margaret expect to gain by bringing Mr. Barry out into the light of day? "He's already murdered one woman, and I'm afraid you might be next."

"I'm not sure why I'm doing it," Margaret said. "Maybe it just seems worthwhile to try to help Dianne. If he knows people are onto him, he'll go away."

"Those kind don't go away, honey, they *get* their way. Dianne's told me all about Cal, and while she's perfectly happy with Charlie, she's clinging to old memories, if you ask me. Why, she came straight out and told me she thought it would be nice to be poor again. Can you imagine any sane person saying that?"

It would be a hard concept for Carolyn Sue to grasp, to be sure.

"She was even saying that her life had more meaning when she and this fellow were struggling to make a life, and then along came that sister of hers, putting the make on the husband, and poor Dianne got backed into a corner."

"She never said much about all this to me," Margaret said. "Why do you suppose she's telling you?"

"Margaret honey, I'm just a motherly old dame that kids feel they can talk to."

Margaret had a hard time imagining the soigné Carolyn Sue, dripping with diamonds and with her every garment labeled with a designer's name, morphing into a motherly old dame, complete with a shoulder to cry on.

"You want to talk to Dianne now?"

"For a minute, please. But wait. Do you know Charles Stark's first wife, Zoe?"

"Hell, yes. Now, she's a handful. Likes her money, but don't we all?"

"She's around New York again, and she's been visiting Charlie."

"He's not goin' to take up with her again, take it from me. She got a whole lot of money when they divorced, and there's no way he's goin' to entangle himself with her again. Lookee, here's Dianne for you."

Dianne sounded subdued. "I'm glad I came," she said, "but I'm worried about Chip and Charlie."

Margaret explained what she was up to, and repeated the answering-machine message. "How do you suppose he knew you'd gone?"

"I was always flying off somewhere when we had a fight or was unhappy about something," Dianne said. "I guess he remembered and figured I'd done it again. But I can't have you doing this, Margaret. He's dangerous."

"He's not going to shoot me," she said, but she wasn't sure at all.

"No, he won't do that again," Dianne said.

"I'm not worried about me, anyhow." She explained her impersonation. "It's you he would be shooting. Is there anything I should be doing or wearing to look more like you? I mean, things he would recognize?"

"Earlier in the year when it was still cool, I used to wear a light pink coat when I went out. It should be hanging in my closet. And those floppy hats that keep the sun off my face."

"I have them both," Margaret said. "And don't worry about Chip. I've been reading to him, and Lourdes is doing fine."

"What about Charlie? I feel terrible about Charlie."

"I haven't seen him today. He went out early. He told Lourdes he'd be back this evening, but he seems to be holding up."

"I'll call him later. He's probably letting Zoe cry on his shoulder or something. What about Gerald?"

"He's been very kind," Margaret said. "And he was glad to help you out."

"But I ran out on him."

"He understands," Margaret said. "Look, I have to get back to your apartment. I'm at my place now. I'll let you know when the coast is clear and you can come home."

Would the coast ever be clear?

Chapter 19

After her phone call to Dallas, Margaret sat quietly in her apartment for a time, thinking. Dianne seemed to be so sure that Cal Barry was aiming for Karen after all. He did know her, but Margaret had assumed he had simply seen a woman resembling Dianne get out of a taxi and had acted. But what reason would he have to kill Dianne's sister?

There was no answer, and she decided to return to the Stark apartment, still pretending to be Dianne. If he knew Dianne was gone, he wouldn't trouble her at all.

The Sunday afternoon streets of Manhattan were empty, and traffic was light. She saw no one resembling Cal Barry lurking or attempting to follow her, so she simply took her usual route toward Fifth Avenue, thinking of Carolyn Sue's comment about Dianne not being over her former husband even after all this time. She'd actually seen him face-to-face not more than a few months ago. Was that when the harassment started? And Dianne claimed to want to be poor again. Did this incomprehensible wish spring from her feelings of worthlessness in the great world of society populated by the likes of Elinor Newhall and Terry Thompson, and indeed, Margaret herself?

She wouldn't be poor if she continued as Charles Stark's

wife. On the other hand, if she found herself again attached to a humble merchant seaman, she wouldn't have a lot of money to worry about. Okay, so assume Dianne had met her ex from time to time, and had given hints that she was longing for the old days, did that turn him into a stalker? Margaret believed that Dianne had been genuinely frightened by that threatening letter, and the idea that someone was watching her. It couldn't all be a sham, especially when Karen's death was as real as Dianne's fear.

Once again, she had to ask why Karen? Karen, who seemed to be interfering with Dianne's present life, and who'd interfered in the past when Dianne was married to Cal Barry. Who had mentioned sibling rivalry? Margaret didn't have much experience in that area, since her brother had merely been an unpleasant boy in the way younger brothers are, and, by virtue of being in line to inherit their father's title, had gotten unfairly (to her mind) preferential treatment.

"Hullo," Margaret said as she passed John on his corner.

"How's it going?"

She stopped. "John, tell me. Did you really see Mrs. Stark talking to the man who lurks around her building?"

"I see a lot of things, but I don't want to get mixed up in that business. Not me. You ask the guy yourself. He's up there across the street."

"I think not," Margaret said. If Cal knew that Dianne had gone away, why was he still hanging about? "John, would you walk with me to the building? He makes me nervous."

"Sure, lady. It's not like I've got meetings with vice presidents I've got to get to."

They strolled toward Fifth, as Margaret took note of the man standing in a doorway across the street.

"I'll be okay now," she said. "It's only a building away." She found a couple of dollars and handed them to John.

"Thanks, but I wasn't doing you a favor for money," he said. "You take care, now." He ambled back to his usual spot, and Margaret proceeded toward the haven of the Starks' building.

She had almost reached the canopy when she felt a hand on her shoulder, and gasped.

"I told you that you can't keep her away from me," said a voice in her ear.

Margaret pulled away from the hand, but he grasped her arm with considerable strength.

"You go in there and call her and tell her to come back now. Or else I'm going to find her and do to her what she wanted done to that bitch sister of hers."

There was no one on the street, and John was probably back on Madison by now. If she could just move a little closer to the front door, the doorman might notice what was happening and frighten him off. She managed to move a couple of feet closer to the door, but still he was holding her arm in a painful grip.

"What do you mean, she wanted her sister to be shot? Is that what you mean?"

She heard an evil chuckle. "When Karen was living with us, she was always prancing around in her nightie and coming on to me, and then she told Dianne that it was me that was after her. That killed everything between us right then. Dianne got on one of those planes, and I didn't see her for a month. Then she got the divorce, even though she didn't want to lose me. I explained what had happened over and over, and when I found her here, living in New York with that rich old guy, I kept trying to see her, to explain that it was Karen's fault. It wasn't until this winter that she started to believe me. I met her on the street, and we talked, and she would have come back to me."

"I don't think she would have left Charlie and her baby." She managed to move them another foot closer to the building.

"Shoulda been our baby," he said. "I make good money now, we coulda had a nice place back in Rhode Island, the way it used to be. She was coming around to my way of thinking, and I knew it would work out. Then I see her sister here, and I think it's perfect. She'll go after the old guy because he's rich, and believe me, Karen liked money. There's no stopping Karen when she puts her mind to something. That would break up Dianne and the old guy. I even saw Karen and the husband together, snuggling up in a taxi once, putting his arm around her."

This didn't sound like the Charles Stark Margaret knew, but she wasn't going to argue the point.

"Dianne knew what was going on. She told me. She told me she wished Karen was dead so she could live a happy life again."

"Mr. Barry, are you telling me you shot Karen Reid because you thought that's what Dianne wanted?"

"It *is* what she wanted. She knew from the time it happened that it was me. She went away so she wouldn't have to tell the cops or anybody. She'd just wait for it to blow over, telling people it was a mugger or something. Everybody would forget the whole thing. And pretty soon we'd be back together."

Margaret thought his reasoning faulty, but she was in no position to dispute him.

"How is it that you have not been caught by the police? A number of people saw the shooting, saw you."

"I've gotten to know the park pretty well, all the places around you can hide. People don't notice guys like me or that guy John on the corner."

"I see. I really must go in," Margaret said. "I'm expecting a call." She pulled her arm from his grasp, catching him unawares, and sprinted toward the building. But he was on her heels and grabbed her again, just as she reached for the door. And wouldn't you know? The doorman wasn't at his desk to notice anything.

"I don't think I can let you go," he said. "I told you what I did, I told you Dianne made me do it. I don't want her to get into trouble. Let's take a walk to the park."

Margaret struggled ineffectively to free herself, but then she grew weak with relief. De Vere was walking briskly, then running down the street from Fifth Avenue. She heard more running footsteps from the other direction, and caught a glimpse of John racing toward her. At the same time a sleek black limousine screeched to a stop in front of the building, and Gerald Toth leapt from the backseat, even as the driver fumbled to get out to open the door.

Overkill on the rescue front, she thought, and felt Cal release her abruptly. She collapsed to her knees, while Cal darted into the street and started running toward Fifth and the park. She hoped De Vere wouldn't take off after him, but would come to her first. She preferred not to be rescued by Gerald Toth. The price of repaying the favor could be too high for her.

As it happened, Gerald and De Vere reached her at the same time. It was John who continued after Cal. Probably just as well. Surely he knew Central Park better than anyone.

"Margaret," the two men said in unison.

"Are you all right? Was that Dianne's stalker?" Gerald said. But it was De Vere who helped her to her feet, and looked at her sternly.

"Well, are you all right?"

"What are you both doing here?" she said.

"Your little friend Paul told me what you were up to," De Vere said, "and I came to save you from whatever peril you were putting yourself in." She looked at him, and although he was scarcely on a par with Gerald in the looks department, he looked very good to her.

"I, too, came to be sure you were not in danger," Gerald said. "The maid or whoever she is at the Starks' said you'd gone out, and I didn't think you should be roaming the streets with that maniac on the loose."

"Who was that fellow that went after him?" De Vere asked.

"An acquaintance," Margaret said. "The man who was holding me is the one who shot Karen. It's Dianne's ex-husband who's been stalking Dianne with the misguided belief that she wanted to reunite with him, and she wanted her sister killed. So he killed her."

"I'll get some people to search the park," De Vere said. "My car is just over on the next block. I'll radio from it. Margaret, you go inside at once and stay there. I'll be with you shortly. You"—he pointed at Gerald—"see that she gets inside safely."

"This is my friend Gerald Toth, Sam. Sam De Vere of the New York Police." The two men nodded warily.

Sam marched away, and Gerald took her arm. "Let's go. You can explain about Dianne when we get upstairs."

Margaret didn't speak in the elevator, but she was thinking that only Paul was missing from her group of heroes.

Chapter 20

*L*ourdes opened the door, looking concerned.

"Mr. Paul telephoned you, Mr. Sam telephoned you, and Mr. Toth telephoned you," she said. "Is there trouble?"

"No," Margaret said. "This is Mr. Toth. Can Lourdes bring you something to drink, Gerald, while I freshen up after my encounter with Mr. Barry?"

"I have coffee already made," Lourdes said. "Go to the drawing room, and I will bring it."

"All right," Gerald said. "You're not going to disappear on me, are you?"

"Me? I've never really cared for Texas, and my current budget won't allow me a trip to England on the spur of the moment. I'll be right with you." Maybe she'd never be able to afford a trip home if Giovanni's decorating skills were rejected by Elinor in favor of Bobby Henley's.

"Sam will probably be joining us after he's called about Barry in the park. I do hope John doesn't get hurt."

"You have the oddest friends, Margaret," Gerald said.

"I don't think of you all as odd," Margaret said sweetly. "Misguided, perhaps. I was quite in control of the situation." She was feeling a bit better about Dianne, in one sense. She probably was no longer in imminent danger of being murdered by Calvin Barry, whose focus now seemed to be on reuniting with her. But the thought of Dianne scheming to have her sister killed. . . . It was all too T. S. Eliot to take in. "Who will rid me of this . . . sister?" It must have been simply a case of wish fulfillment on the part of Barry. That's what he wanted her to say, and he was all too willing to comply with what he thought he heard.

Margaret brushed her hair and washed her face. Then she changed her slacks, which had been dirtied when she went to her knees. She looked at the pink coat she'd tossed on a chair. Her misguided and unnecessary attempt to don a disguise.

Gerald was peacefully sipping coffee and sampling some of the housekeeper's prized cookies when she joined him in the drawing room. Chip's playpen was there, but he was not.

"What exactly was all that about? What's everything been about these past few days?" Gerald asked. "The only thing I know for certain is that not all the deranged people of the world have migrated to California."

"No, we still have our share here," Margaret said. She set about trying to explain what she believed had been unfolding.

"So sweet Dianne hates her society-lady life with all the good things that money can buy. I never knew a woman who felt that way. I don't suppose she's about to leave her husband to prove that she can do without."

"I think not," Margaret said. "When she talked about going back to work with the airlines, she concluded that she couldn't leave Charlie and Chip, and I really don't think she has any attachment to Barry; it was just the idea of a poor and simple life that attracted her."

"But was her sister such a threat that she would see her dead?"

"Not a threat, but maybe a reminder of the role—real or imagined—that she'd played in destroying the poor and simple life Dianne had had. And look, she was possibly going to destroy the rich and complicated life Dianne had now. Although I suppose one would have to ask Charlie about that, if one dared. I don't."

They heard the house phone, and soon the doorbell, and Sam De Vere joined them, looking quite unlike a policeman recently in pursuit of a murderer. Or perhaps he hadn't done any pursuing himself. He wore his usual pressed jeans and polished loafers, and an unwrinkled blue dress shirt, tieless naturally, with the sleeves slightly rolled. In contrast, Gerald had on the expensive shoes the waiter at the d'Este had noticed, a well-cut pale yellow linen jacket, and tan trousers with a crease that could cut steel.

Margaret smiled at De Vere. "What's the news?"

"The guys seem to have located Barry on the other side of the park. They grabbed him just when he was strolling out into the traffic around Columbus Circle like he was on his way someplace for cocktail hour."

Margaret's and Gerald's eyes met briefly. Surely Barry wasn't planning on dining at Jean-Georges.

"He'll be questioned, and we'll have to get Dianne back here to give us some information. Paul told me where she was," he said to Margaret's questioning look. "I spoke to Carolyn Sue and told her to keep tabs on Dianne for a day or so, and then we'll want her back. I may send you to fetch her, because I don't want her deciding to run off again."

"Carolyn Sue said she wouldn't let Dianne come back

until you said it was all right," Margaret said. "You're the only person she trusts."

"I don't understand," Gerald said.

"Trusting De Vere? Carolyn Sue Hoopes is a Texas lady who's a good judge of character. She knows he's about the best there is for . . . for getting a person sewn up," Margaret said. "More coffee?"

"I'd like you to go tomorrow," Sam said.

"All right, I can arrange it," Margaret said.

"But we're having dinner," Gerald said.

"Police business," Margaret said. "I'm afraid I can't deny the coppers just for the sake of dinner with you. You do understand, don't you?"

Margaret noticed that De Vere was, for a change, paying close attention to their talk.

"I do understand," Gerald said. "It's a very worthwhile thing you're doing, helping a friend. We'll dine another time, although it will have to be soon. I've got to get back to California in a week's time, or my hard-won empire may be overcome by computerized barbarians."

"Gerald has a computer business," Margaret explained, and when she named it, De Vere's eyes widened. He must read the financial pages cast aside by Paul.

"We'll do something when I get back from Dallas," Margaret said. "Elinor will be sorry to see you leave New York. And Leila, too, I imagine."

"I've seen quite enough of both of them," he said. "There's only one person I regret I haven't seen enough of."

"If you'll excuse Margaret and me," De Vere said, "I need to speak to her privately about what went on downstairs. While it's fresh in her mind."

His tone was so mild that Gerald couldn't take offense,

so he finished his coffee and stood up. "Promise to call me as soon as you're back with Dianne. I really should take her out someplace nice, too. After what she's been through."

Then he turned those fabulous blue eyes on Margaret and kind of winked.

"I'll be back soon," she said, and he had scarcely left the room before De Vere had her in his arms whispering, "You trying to get yourself killed? I don't handle jealousy well."

"You don't have any call to be jealous, Sam. He's just a friend."

"A very rich, handsome friend. I want you on a plane tomorrow morning, and back here by the day after."

"Yessir. Done."

"And I don't expect you to lose Dianne along the way. She's got a lot to answer for."

"You surely don't think she actually asked Barry to kill Karen, do you?"

"I think that's kind of his defense. Her obedient servant, only doing his job."

"Charlie is going to be so hurt by this," Margaret said. "He just adores her."

There was a gentle knock on the drawing room door, and Lourdes came in. "Mrs. Stark, Mrs. Zoe is here. I told her Mr. Stark was not in and that Mrs. Stark, the other one, was away, but she wanted to speak to you."

"Me?" Margaret was surprised. "I don't know the woman."

After a minute or two, Lourdes showed Zoe Stark into the drawing room, although presumably she knew the way perfectly well, since this had once been her home.

"Lady Margaret, what a pleasure. I don't think we've

met, since I moved away about the time you arrived, I should think. But we have so many mutual friends . . ." She eyed De Vere, who said, "I will be in touch with you shortly, Lady Margaret. So nice to have seen you."

He departed without waiting or wanting to be introduced to Zoe. And when he called her Lady Margaret, she knew she definitely didn't want his association with the police to be mentioned. So Margaret simply pretended he hadn't been there, and asked Zoe to sit, have coffee, and get on with what she wanted to say.

"I know you're a good friend of Dianne's," Zoe said. She had a throaty voice, strenuously cultured, and she looked as good as reports of her had had it. Unless you had Margaret's sharp eyes, you couldn't really tell that she'd had a few tucks taken. "Lady Margaret, I am deeply concerned about this business of a stalker. It's taken a great toll on Charles, who will always be a very important person to me. We were married for a number of years, and I am the mother of his son and daughter. Dianne is an entirely unsuitable wife for a man of his position and consequence. It might have been better for everyone if Calvin had managed to shoot the right person."

Margaret was briefly appalled, then she was interested. What was this woman up to?

"If I am such a friend of Dianne's, why on earth are you saying such things to me?"

"Charles and I have had several long discussions lately. He is not as content in his life as he would like to be, and I would hope that for his sake and Dianne's you would encourage her to think about taking another path through life."

"Impossible!" Margaret said. "And what do you know

about Calvin?" Margaret would have thought the only Calvin Zoe would be aware of was Calvin Klein.

Zoe dismissed the question with a wave of her hand, but Margaret persisted. "I must know immediately." She sat up straight and looked Zoe in the eye. Aristocratic disdain had a way of working well with pretentious Americans.

"I . . . I met him a few years ago," Zoe said. "It was just after Dianne and Charles married, and apparently he was tracking her down. I hadn't yet moved to Seattle. I was still known as Zoe Stark, so in his search for the new Mrs. Stark, he found me. We found we had mutual interests. Charles had abandoned me, and Dianne had abandoned Calvin. Fortunately, I had William in the wings, a very attractive young man with whom I intended to be very happy in spite of what Charles had done to me. I was going to get even. That's all. We kept in touch even after I moved away."

Margaret closed her eyes. This affair was becoming fairly Byzantine. "Did you encourage Calvin to seek revenge?"

"Of course not. I merely suggested that he could make himself feel better by . . . by making her feel worse in her present marriage. He got the idea of stalking her himself, without any help from me, although I personally hoped that her fear would drive her away from New York."

"But you didn't suggest that he actually kill her, or kill her sister."

"I said not."

Margaret wondered whether anyone else would appear to confess to driving Calvin Barry to greater heights of terrorism.

"What is it you say you want me to do?" Margaret asked.

"Convince Dianne to leave this life and Charles. Find someone more suitable, or stand by Calvin and see him through the mess he's made. I thought I had made that clear."

Margaret had no answer. She was beginning to feel a little sorry for Cal, who sounded like he was a tennis ball in the courts of some pretty weird women, including Dianne.

"I think that is up to Dianne, not me," Margaret said. "I refuse to become involved in her personal life."

"What kind of friend are you?"

"Better than I thought," Margaret said.

Chapter 21

Margaret's flight to Dallas on Monday morning arrived at one o'clock. The cowboy-esque chauffeur was waiting for her. She had rather hoped that Carolyn Sue would bring Dianne to the airport, packed and ready to fly, so that they could simply board the next flight back to New York. But Carolyn Sue insisted that Margaret come to the ranch and stay the night. They could go back to New York in the morning. "I'll see if Ben can let you have the company jet. It would be so much nicer than a commercial flight," Carolyn Sue said. As Margaret had noted, the appeal of great wealth is highly seductive, and the thought of a flight to oneself is whipped cream on the cake.

So Margaret rolled up to the huge house, and was ushered into the white-on-white living room. Even she was impressed by the grandfather clock.

"Margaret honey, you're lookin' terrific!" Carolyn Sue was not in white herself, but wore a jacket and slacks with an odd silvery sheen. Margaret thought she'd seen the clothes in a Ralph Lauren ad.

"You look fine yourself," Margaret said. "Where's Dianne?"

"That poor child. She just sits in her room crying her eyes out. Even though I told her she was going home to see her little boy, that didn't stop the waterworks from flowin'. They catch that devil of a husband of hers?"

"De Vere has matters well in hand, but he does need to talk to her."

"Sam is a wonder. I just love that boy. When you two goin' to get hitched? It's about time."

"Carolyn Sue, after what I've seen of married and post-married life lately, I'm not sure I have the strength for it."

"I know he's not rich like . . . like that fellow Dianne was telling me about, Gerald Toth, but you're not goin' to find a finer man than Sam De Vere, rich or poor."

"I know you're seriously infatuated by him," Margaret said, "and I entirely agree that he's a fine person, but . . ."

"No buts here or there or anywhere. Mr. Sanchez, will you have somebody go knock on Mrs. Stark's door and ask her to join us?"

A butler-like person that Margaret hadn't noticed hovering in a corner scurried to do the mistress's bidding.

"I was thinkin' of havin' a big barbecue tonight to welcome you to Texas," Carolyn Sue said, "but I decided it wouldn't be any fun without Paul and Sam here, and even old Ben, who's over in Houston on business. Don't worry, he didn't take the plane. I'll ask him tonight when he gets home to fly you two back to New York."

"Margaret! You're here!" Dianne seemed surprised to see her.

"Of course I'm here. De Vere must have told you I was coming to bring you back to New York."

"I knew I was supposed to go back, but . . . do I really have to?"

"You really do. And you're not going to try to run away again, are you?"

"No. That was stupid. I was just so upset about Karen,

and everything. I didn't want to get shot down on the street."

"Calvin would never have shot you," Margaret said. "And he only shot Karen because you wanted him to."

Dianne hung her head. "You know about that? I didn't really tell him to shoot her, I just said I'd be better off without her. I guess he wanted to prove his love for me, as if murder was the way to a woman's heart. But, Margaret, I don't want to go back to him, I never did. I want to stay with Charlie and Chip. If what it takes is working on those damned committees, that's what I'll do. But I'm going to find someplace to do real charity work, a hospital or a place that helps children learn to read, anything. And I never want my name to appear in Poppy Dill's column ever again."

"I'm sure Poppy will agree to that."

"And I don't want anything bad to happen to Cal."

"That's why you have to go back to New York. He'll have to pay some kind of price for shooting Karen, but if you can convince the authorities that he mistakenly thought it would bring you back to him, perhaps the price won't be as high as it would be for cold-blooded murder."

"I don't think I can convince the authorities of that," Dianne said, and suddenly looked enormously weary and even (perish the thought) much older.

"Why not?"

"Because it wasn't that way at all."

Margaret and Carolyn Sue waited as she gathered her thoughts and finally spoke again.

"It wasn't that way," she said at last. "I told him to kill her. I begged him to do it. I must have been crazy, after the way he was harassing me and tormenting me, but when I finally saw him that last time, I told him that everything in my life had been horrible since we parted, not Charlie and Chip, but all the rest of the stuff I was expected to do, and now here was Karen making it worse, just being there, flirting with Charlie as if I wasn't around, spending his money as if it was her right. I just told him to do it. I didn't believe he'd actually go through with it, but he did."

"Then why did you run away? He wasn't a threat to you."

"I thought you'd understand how it was," Dianne said. "You're my best friend, and you know what I'm thinking practically. I ran partly to make people believe I was still afraid, but mostly I ran because even if I didn't pull the trigger, I was guilty of killing my sister."

"What they goin' to do to that poor child?" Carolyn Sue asked.

"It seems rather murky," Margaret said. "She didn't kill Karen, and what sister or brother hasn't had even vaguely murderous thoughts about a troublesome sibling one time or another, and even expressed them aloud. And I still think Calvin wanted to kill Dianne all along, to erase her from his life. He must have been a little crazy, as the stalking indicates. That takes a rather twisted mind. I prefer to think that Karen was just a case of mistaken identity. And if anyone fixes blame on Dianne, it should be shared with Zoe. She was putting ideas into Cal's head as well."

"It sure is a different world from when I was a girl," Carolyn Sue said. "Well, you'll get her back to New York, and then you can relax and start thinking about marrying Sam."

"I don't think so," Margaret said, but the thought was

genuinely pleasing. A nice but not uncomplicated life with Sam De Vere was worth a lot more than all the luxury Gerald Toth could shower on her. She couldn't imagine Gerald being content with a Chinese take-out dinner. He'd probably feel it necessary to buy the restaurant.

Carolyn Sue pouted. She'd already offered to stage-manage a wedding for Margaret. She was keen on pulling together major events, and Margaret was her last hope. She said she'd been told by Paul not even to think about any such thing for him if he and Georgina decided to wed.

"Don't worry," Margaret said. "It's something I'm going to think very seriously about . . . later."

"But what is poor Dianne going to do with her life?"

"Remember, she told us she was going back to Charlie and Chip, and she'd find something genuinely worthwhile to do. I believe she will. You don't have to wear a designer frock to do good. Maybe I'll join her. Charlie was making the funeral arrangements for Karen. There's to be a service as soon as Dianne gets back to New York, and once that's over, I think Dianne will be on the way to putting her life back together."

"That's all well and good," Carolyn Sue said, "but I still think you need to make some decisions about your own life."

"I will," Margaret said, "but first I have to get to work on Elinor Newhall and persuade her to hire Giovanni Millennia to redecorate her house in the Hamptons. And then I've got a pile of envelopes to address—for a worthwhile cause."

A PERFECT DAY FOR DYING

A posh party in the Caribbean arranged by one of Lady Margaret Priam's good friends results in a murder, and Lady Margaret finds herself flying to the scene to pose as a partygoer. Her snooping uncovers messy little secrets from the past, as black-mail, black magic, and deadly rumors expose the dark side of paradise.

MOURNING GLORIA

With a face-lift, a new husband, and plans for a major social comeback, Gloria Anton is back in town—until she tumbles to her death down the back stairs of an old East Side mansion. Lady Margaret is intrigued by this tragedy, because it mirrors another death in the same setting forty years ago . . .

by JOYCE CHRISTMAS

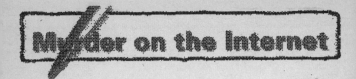

A FÊTE WORSE THAN DEATH

When a nosy self-proclaimed public relations specialist is strangled right before one of her own soirées, Lady Margaret Priam takes an instant interest in the case. Even with danger at every turn, Lady Margaret is determined to discover . . . whodunit.

A STUNNING WAY TO DIE

Lady Margaret Priam is interrupted during a party by a phone call from a friend—who has a dead woman in his antiques shop. When her friend becomes the prime suspect, Lady Margaret decides to find out the truth, and her investigation takes her into the glitzy social circles of Hollywood.

by JOYCE CHRISTMAS

FRIEND OR FAUX

Lady Margaret Priam returns to her family's castle in England to escape the boredom of a Manhattan summer season—and to deal with the murder of one of her brother's houseguests. A whiz at solving murders in the past, even Lady Margaret is stunned by the goings-on at home.

IT'S HER FUNERAL

A neighborhood busybody—known for opposing the construction of a new luxury high-rise—is found dead, and Lady Margaret Priam is called in by the construction company's owner to calm local fears. But she is soon up to her neck in unexpected trouble.

by JOYCE CHRISTMAS

Published by Fawcett Gold Medal.
Available at your local bookstore.